Strange Stories for

Ordinary People

By: Heather Veley

I dedicate this book to everyone in my life who encouraged me on the good days and were my rock for the bad ones. Thank you for keeping me sane.

Table of Contents

The Morning After-	1
What sits in the corner-	2
Frozen Eyes-	5
The Safe-	14
Chatting in the Attic-	18
Tar-	22
The Horror Muse-	25
Movie Date-	44
True Love's Release-	53
A Winter Scene-	66
The Boatman-	70
A Night on the Town-	76
Brand New Thing-	87
Morning Routine-	89
Campfire Stories-	92
The Talk-	106
Human_Conscious.exe-	108
Down the Sewer Hole-	112
The Dancing Cat-	129
The Romantic-	135
Searching for Peace-	141
Bump in the Night-	153

The Morning After

She walks down the country road, with blood-soaked hair and red eyes. All night she had been running. Running away from the dark heart of the forest. Her shoes came off a long time ago, allowing her bare feet to be scrapped and scratched. Her dress, once clean and modest, is now torn nearly to ribbons. She doesn't say a word as she moves, her voice had given out long ago. She lost it from her screaming throughout the night.

The sun starts to come up. Its orange rays touch the roofs of the town ahead of her. The citizens will soon wake up, eat breakfast, and go to work. Just like they've done so many times before. They will not expect her silent arrival. They will not expect her blank, soulless stare. She will pass the drug store and the church before they stop her. They will ask her many questions.

"Who are you?"

"Where did you come from?"

"What happened to you?"

But she won't be able to answer them. How could she? How could she put to words the horrors she's seen? How could she describe the evil the lives deep within the forest? All the flesh that has been torn apart and all the blood that has been spilled. All the bones that've been smashed to bits or turned into appliances. And the smiles; those wide, cruel smiles. Their owners without any human empathy, only sadistic glee.

How could she explain any of that?

In ten minutes, she will be in that spot. She will stare ahead like she had done for hours. The citizens will plead and beg for answers. But for now, she walks in silence. The violent tornado is behind her, but she will forever bear the damage it had done.

What sits in the corner

The morning started out rather nice for Megan. Her alarm went off at the usual time and she didn't feel the least bit groggy. After a few sips of water and tackling a few levels of her favorite puzzle game, she felt ready to get up, and it only took her ten minutes. There was even enough time for her to use the toilet before breakfast. Even the bags under her eyes weren't as dark as usual. It looked like it was going to be a good day.

She shuffled down the short hallway then turned into the kitchen. It was a small room but perfectly fine for her. Out of muscle memory, she turned on the light above the sink then the coffee maker, just like every other morning. It crackled as it spit out the hot drink into the pot. She then grabbed a cereal bar to eat while she waited for it to brew.

About halfway through her meal, she heard an unfamiliar gurgle and paused to listen. It wasn't coming from the five-year-old coffee pot, and it certainly wasn't coming from her. The gurgle happened again; it was coming from behind her. A gross chill went up her spine as she turned her head towards the living room. The kitchen light only reached out so far and with it being four in the morning, her window wasn't very helpful. By the time she did a one-eighty, the sound had stopped. She was about to write it off as exhausted paranoia when something moved from behind the wall where her couch was. The gross chill returned as she crept around the corner.

It was difficult to make out anything in the dark, but she could see its general form. A large, fleshy mass bulging out from the corner of the room, nearly consuming the couch. It expanded and deflated like an exposed lung. The kitchen light reflected on several shining orbs all around its body. It's eyes? Before Megan could focus enough to tell, she noticed more movement coming from the ceiling. Several thin tentacles swayed and reached out as far as they could without leaving the corner. "It" was exploring what it could.

Megan ducked behind the wall; she saw enough. The small cereal bar curdled in her stomach. Part of her wanted to turn on the lights to see what it was but the urge to throw up kept her still. It was possible that it was a hallucination; she had been working a lot of double shifts recently. But why did it seem so real?

Once the initial shock dissipated, she slowly walked back to the kitchen counter where the coffee maker waited patiently for her. Her body went into autopilot, filling a travel mug with coffee and turning off the machine before heading back down the hallway to the bathroom. Several times in her routine, her subconscious tried to redirect her thoughts to whatever was in the next room and how she should deal with it. However, she refused to dwell on it, focusing instead on making sure each tooth was flossed before brushing.

Minutes later, she returned to the kitchen in her work uniform. The gurgling from the thing caught her attention, but it was again blocked out to focus on the task at hand. She grabbed her lunch from the fridge and fastened the lid onto the travel mug. Then she turned to face the dark living room. The front door was on the other side, past the couch. Her stomach did a flip thinking about the tentacles grabbing onto her or feeling its gaze. She took a deep breath and started walking.

It knew she was there. She knew it knew. She could feel every one of its beady eyes on her as she exited the kitchen. The gurgling stopped momentarily but picked up once she was half-way across the room. She heard it shift slightly but kept her eyes glued to the exit in front of her. Just as she went to reach for the doorknob, she heard something long and slimy approach. It was ear level and slithering closer. She ducked before it could get her and fumbled with the lock until she managed to open the door wide enough to slip out.

She slammed the door shut and locked it with a shaky hand then sped down the hall. There was some stirring in the apartment immediately next to hers, but she didn't stop. She trotted to the elevator and hopped on. Only when the doors closed did she finally let out a sigh. Her mind finally allowed her to question everything she had seen. What was that thing? How did it get into her apartment? How long had it been sitting there? What did it want from her?

Try as she might, she could not come up with an answer. None of it made sense and she feared investigating any further. The elevator chimed and opened its doors to let her out. There was only one other person in the small lobby, the cleaning lady getting ready to start her shift. The idea to tell her everything popped into Megan's mind, but she stopped. Who was going to believe that there is currently a giant tentacle monster sitting in the corner of her living room? The more she thought about it, the more ridiculous it sounded. So, she passed the cleaning lady without uttering a word.

Before she knew it, she was in her car, driving to work. Twice she had to shake her head to make sure this was real life. The steering wheel felt the same, and there weren't any differences in her route. Megan stopped at a red light, staring straight ahead. It could be possible that the creature she saw was just her imagination. It was early in the morning; she could have hallucinated it in her drowsy state. The more she thought about it, the more reasonable it sounded.

      The light turned green, and she pressed the gas. Certainly, of course. It all made perfect sense. When she goes home after her shift, the thing won't be there because it doesn't exist. It never existed. This was all her brain playing tricks on her. Megan smiled in relief as she pulled into the parking lot to start her day.

Frozen Eyes

The first thing Daniel noticed about Sherwood Avenue was how quiet it was. Even as the city bus steamed and creaked away, the area was quiet. People hurried between the local shops, picking up last-minute birthday gifts or some bread from the tiny bakery. There was one break in the peace when a mother dragged her screaming toddler out of the coffee shop while holding another child on her hip. A jogger dashed past him with earbuds in. He wanted to trip the guy mid-stride, but the idea came too late for him to act.

A dark cloud hovered above the street, pushing away the yellow sunlight. The looming threat of showers that were predicted on the news inched forward unrelentingly. People were now scattering to find shelter to protect their purchases. Their frenzy made Daniel grin, even chuckle a bit. He imagined the old lady carrying the birthday cake tripping and splattering it all over the sidewalk before she got to car. Or the bearded idiot with sunglasses getting caught in the downpour and ruining his new shoes. The thought tickled him pink.

As much as he wanted to stay to watch the inevitable slapstick comedy, he had someplace to be. He pulled out his phone and entered an address into the map app; his knuckles still tingled from his 'acquisition' of it. In a moment, a blue line marked his path. The sky grew darker as a few drops hit the ground and he sped off. It didn't take long before he was across the street from a tall tan building. The outside was immaculate with freshly power-washed bricks and neatly trimmed bushes in the front. It was nice, far nicer than his place. That got his blood boiling. He put his phone back in his pocket and stormed over. The tiny sprinkling turned into larger water droplets that smacked his head and splattered onto the road.

To his relief, the front door had a little green awning for him to take shelter under. However, the moment he looked to the side of the door; his confidence dropped. A long list of names corresponding with a line of white buttons was displayed off to the side. He gripped the doorknob to turn it, but it wouldn't budge. He swore under his breath.

"Of course, she would get an apartment where you had to be buzzed in."

He scanned the list and her name jumped out to him. Part of him wanted to press the button to talk to her right there but reason stopped him.

There was no way she would let him in. Plan B began to form. Again, he scanned the list for another name, one that looked naïve and trusting. He spotted one and pressed the buzzer. No response. He pressed again but nothing. Daniel grumbled as he looked for another name. Just as he was about to make his next selection, the speaker crackled.

"Hello? Who is this?" An old woman asked.

Daniel sighed in relief and pressed the intercom button.

"Sorry! I'm trying to get to my friend's apartment but he's not letting me in. I don't think he can hear me. Can you buzz me in so I can get out of the rain?"

More heavy raindrops started to fall, making loud splashes behind him. He made sure to hold the intercom long enough for the woman to hear.

"Oh, certainly dearie! Give me one second."

A loud buzzing noise came from the door, and he pulled it open. He slipped in quietly then rushed over to the stairs close by. Each step he took echoed loudly no matter how lightly he put his foot on the tile. When he got to the third floor, it was silent. There weren't any sounds of domestic bustling or even a TV playing a game show. Perfect, he needed the privacy. A few steps into the hall and he was at the door number on the address. Daniel took a second to straighten his ruffled appearance before knocking.

"Hold on a second," a familiar voice called from the other side.

For the first time in a while, Daniel felt his heart skip. It had been days since he heard that voice; he thought he would never hear it again after that night. He waited patiently as small footsteps pattered towards him and the lock clicked as it was turned. The door cracked open slightly then was pushed out farther. A few long strands of blonde hair swung out from the opening followed by the thin wire frames of a large pair of glasses. Then a face poked out, her face. Pale and thin and discolored by a deep purple bruise swelling on her cheek. Daniel winced just looking at it. She looked down the hall then forward. The moment she locked eyes with him, she pulled the door to shut it, but he caught it in time.

"Go away!" She screamed.

"Angie, baby, just give me a minute!" He pleaded as calmly as he could.

"No! Go away!" She cried, "I don't want to see you again!"

"Angie, please! Just let me explain! Can we talk?"

"I've got nothing to say to you! Go away or I'll call the cops!"

The door started to slip through his fingers. Fury rose within him, but he suppressed it. He needed to keep his cool; he needed to work his way in. Tears were quickly whipped up and he peered around the closing crack with the most pathetic face he could put on.

"Angie, baby, please," he begged.

She glanced up. There was fear in her eyes but he could feel the pressure on the door weaken. After a short standoff, she opened the door wide enough for him.

"Ten minutes," she spat.

Daniel slipped inside as she shut the door behind him. There was nowhere for her to go now. The thought almost made him smile but he kept the stern look on his face. Angie shuffled past him through the hallway leading towards the living room. The journey was cramped by cardboard boxes on both sides; some empty, some not. He peered into the ones that were open and spotted a few items that had 'disappeared' from their apartment.

Clothes, pictures, and stupid trinkets that she would find at a crappy yard sale. She told him her parents were holding onto them until they moved into the new place she was nagging him to look at. He believed her at the time, then smacked her for not talking to him first. Even their bookshelf from the TV room now stood at the end of the hall, holding an assortment of new crap and books. His anger from her deception rose until he noticed what was on top of the bookshelf and his blood went cold.

Sitting in a frilly pink dress with its arms in its lap was a black-haired porcelain doll. Its eyes were fixed on him; its hollow stare made him shiver. A large crack ran from the peak of its brow to its chin. He remembered that one. He found it sitting on the kitchen table one day. Angie begged him to let her keep it, even in her corner of the bedroom where he wouldn't see it. He hated dolls; hated them for as long as he could remember. She should have remembered that. He had no idea she kept the pieces from when he threw it against the wall or that she put them back together. Now those same painted eyes examined him again, almost mockingly. He slowly slid up against the wall and rounded the corner.

When he made it to the living room his stomach bottomed out. All around the room there were dozens of dolls of all sizes and types, boxed and unboxed, wearing a variety of outfits. Pirates, cowboys, princesses, and even Nuns. He recognized a few of them from when Angie tried to sneak into their apartment; they all had cracked faces like the one on the bookshelf. Most of them were new. He even spotted some clowns in the colorful crowd which gave him the creeps. She couldn't have bought them all in the week she was gone.

As he inched his way into the room, he felt an animosity around him. It felt like all their dead eyes glared at him, letting him know he wasn't welcomed. Angie was already sitting on an old sofa by the windows, something he remembered from her parent's house that was supposed to go to their new apartment. On the coffee table in front of her lay a doll in a star-covered wizard robe and white beard with some glue and repair tools next to it. It too had a crack running down its face. He stood next to the couch until Angie looked at him with a raised eyebrow and he sat down stiffly.

"Alright, talk," she said coldly.

A lump formed in Daniel's throat. He had to pick his words carefully but the continued stares from the dolls were making him nervous. After a moment of imagining them gone, he spoke.

"Baby, I think you're overreacting-"

"To what, exactly?" she shot back, her words as icy as liquid nitrogen.

"Baby, listen, I know it's been a rough couple of months, but work has been stressing me out and you know how I get when I'm stressed."

"I know."

She rubbed her bruised cheek. Daniel swallowed hard. This was going to be tricky.

"Angie, I'm so sorry. It's just that... I've had so much on my mind, and you were in my way at the time," he paused to gage her body language. She wasn't making eye contact. "I didn't want to hit you; it was an accident. I swear it won't happen again."

"Reusing that line, huh?"

The response came down on him like a sledgehammer. Angie kept looking at the wizard doll in front of her and reaching out to fix the wrinkles in its robe. Daniel rushed to think of something, anything. There was still one card he had yet to play, it had to work. He practiced the line in his head a few times then reached over to take her hand. It stiffened up in his grip and she finally looked up at him with worried eyes. He pulled it up and clasped it between his palms then blinked a few times to make his eyes look watery.

"Angie, I know we've had it rough...but it's going to be better.... I can promise you that! You're the best thing that's happened to me in a long time and I wouldn't be the same if I lost you.... So, Angie," he stopped for dramatic effect, "Will you marry me?"

The expression that appeared on her face was not what he expected; it was a mix of bewilderment and disgust. After some silence, she yanked her hand out of his oyster grasp then walked into the center of the room, facing away from him.

"It's over Daniel," she said slowly, "We're not getting back together this time."

With each word that came out of her mouth, Daniel felt his chest squeeze harder and harder.

"But-.... Baby, we can work this out! I'll do anything to keep you with me! We can go to that counselor you've been talking about. We can-"

"That's not going to fix anything and you know it!"

The thunder in her voice shook some of the items next to the wizard doll, or at least it seemed like it. Daniel didn't know she could shout like that at all. They went silent again. After some time, she spoke.

"After my lease is up, I'm moving to Colorado. My dad has a few properties out there so I can have a fresh start. Rebecca will be over soon to help me unpack more. Please leave now."

The final nail in the coffin, nothing left to say. Daniel blinked as the last three words played back in his mind. His shoulders sank and he couldn't even shift in his seat. He could feel the eyes of the dolls on him as if they were laughing at him. Then his gaze went to her waist. So many times, he held onto those curves to keep her close; now they were out of his reach forever. On that thought, he stood up. Part of him wanted to storm out despite the pouring rain that drowned out all sound. But another part of him had a different idea. He crept around the table, heading right for her. When he was only a foot away, she turned around and her eyes widened.

"N-"

His fist made contact with her face before she could cry out. The force knocked her to the ground as her glasses skittered under a nearby chair. A small whimper escaped her mouth as she tried to comprehend what was going on. He didn't give her the chance as he jumped on top of her to pin her down. His fingers wrapped around her neck and squeezed with every ounce of strength he had. Her fingernails clawed his hands as she tried to escape, drawing blood. He ignored it and squeezed her scrawny neck, watching her pale face go from pink to red then eventually purple. At one point, her hands froze over his knuckles as she choked and gurgled and he watched her body go limp. Five more minutes went by before he finally let go. Angry red marks appeared on her neck while her face was forever frozen in shock.

He stood up and inhaled deeply, the weight on his shoulders was gone. Then he looked around at the dolls still staring at him. There was no anger or smugness on their faces, just painted on eyes and mouths. His gaze stopped on one of the clown dolls in a pink and purple jumpsuit with matching cap. It was exactly the type of thing Angie would have gone for. He moseyed over to the thing and picked it up. It was stiff from age and smelled like the inside of an old woman's house. Without a second thought he chucked it against the wall. The porcelain head shattered to bits as the body fell to the ground with a 'thunk'. Outside, a loud clap of thunder boomed, and the lamp light flickered.

Adrenaline rushed through his system as he looked around for other things to smash. The little girl wearing a white dress, the little boy in the sailor outfit, the weird harlequin with the huge nose. All were fair game. His hatred and fear turned into giddiness. Before he could get started with his rampage, a sudden thought surfaced. Rebecca will be over soon, and he didn't know how soon. He shook the jitters from his hands and turned to leave but stopped in his tracks.

Standing upright in the opening of the hallway was the doll in the frilly pink dress, her painted eyes staring at him blankly. The animosity he sensed before slowly returned but was mixed with white-hot rage. David heard shuffling behind him and turned to see the other dolls had stood up as well. His stomach turned as he frantically looked around in disbelief. Suddenly, he felt a sharp pain in the back of his ankle, and he screamed. He looked down to see one of the sailor boys clasped onto his leg, stabbing a seam ripper into his tendon. Then it looked up at him. Its face was stuck in a painted expression, but its eyes shined in an almost human way.

"How dare you!" A small voice cried.

Daniel screamed again. He kicked the doll off and it landed on some of its brethren, but didn't shatter like the other one. Instead, it stood back up while some of the others crowded around him. Daniel turned to run but his foot stopped midair and he fell on his face. Looking back, he saw that his shoelaces had been tied together. He tried to crawl away, but the dolls dogpiled him and dragged him backwards. They pulled him to the edge of the coffee table then flipped him onto his back, pinning him to the ground.

The doll in the pink dress climbed on top of him. Daniel attempted to throw her off, but she was as heavy as a real person. As he struggled to break free, he heard more voices all around him.

"This can't be happening!"

"Someone find help! She may still be alive!"

"It's no use! She's gone!"

"How will we survive now?"

"Hold his head and I'll slit his throat!"

"WAIT!"

They all turned to the coffee table where the wizard doll stood. Daniel's heart sunk.

"Death would be an easy escape for him," the wizard's words boomed, "I have a better idea. Hold him still."

. . .

"So, what do we have here?" Detective Baxter asked as he pushed aside the police tape on the apartment door.

Officer Finn waited for him in the hall while the forensics team bustled to gather evidence. The two slid past them to reach the living room where three men zipped up a body bag to be carried out.

"We got the call from a friend of the victim. She was coming over to help Angela Smith unpack from her recent move and found the door unlocked. When she came in, she found her dead on the floor. Cause of death is strangulation," Officer Finn paused as the detective pulled out a pen and pad. When Baxter was caught up, he nodded, "From the looks of it, there's no sign of forced entry but there was a struggle once the perp was inside. We found this."

He reached over to a sealed baggie on the coffee table and held it up. Inside was a seam ripper with blood on the tip. Baxter examined it then scribbled something on his pad.

"Do we have a suspect?" He asked.

"The witness told us she believes the killer is the victim's ex-boyfriend, Daniel Ross. According to her, she helped Angela move out of their shared apartment to escape him. We have a couple reports of domestic disturbances he's perpetrated within the last six months, but the charges were dropped by the victim. The theory is that he found out where she was and came over to convince her to get back together. Clearly, that's not how it ended. I have officers going to the suspect's address and we're working on getting an arrest warrant."

"Where is the witness?"

"She's at the station now to give a full statement. The victim's parents have been contacted and they're on their way there."

"Got any other clues."

"Not yet. I'm gonna let the boys comb over the place a little longer. It's strange though."

"How so?"

"I mean, aside from the body and little bit of blood, the place looks clean. Nothing was taken from the apartment either."

Detective Baxter paused to look around.

"Huh. You're right. That is bizarre," he agreed.

He jotted down a few notes then tucked his pen and pad away.

"Ugh, they're so creepy," Officer Finn muttered as he looked around, "These dolls. I don't know what it is about them but they're so freaky. Especially the clowns."

"My wife collects them."

"Really? How do you live with it?"

"Easy. They make her happy and they don't move."

Officer Finn nodded. He was about to leave when he spotted something. His eyes narrowed to look into the inanimate crowd then he recoiled.

"Eh! That one!" He scoffed.

"Which one?"

"That one!"

Officer Finn pointed to a doll sitting between a wizard and a Southern belle in pink. It was dressed in modern clothes and had an uncannily realistic face with glassy eyes. Detective Baxter backed off and turned to the hall.

"Okay, THAT one is creepy," he agreed, "Come on, let's go meet with the parents to get their statements."

They hurried out, leaving the techs to continue brushing for fingerprints. Hours went by before they finally packed up their equipment to return to the station. When the door to the apartment closed, the whispers started up. Sunlight disappeared through the window blinds as the dolls continued to stare off into space with their froze eyes.

The Safe

Jeremy sat on the basement floor exasperated with several tools around him. Despite their quality, none of them were useful for the job that sat across from their owner: a dusty safe the size of an old television. Judging by the amount of rust and grime on its surface, had been down there for a very long time. There was a dial on it, but it was useless without the combination. Jeremy stared at the giant hunk of metal for a few more minutes before standing to go upstairs.

As soon as he got to the top, the afternoon sun hit him. He sidestepped the boxes full of cookware and picture frames to get to the master bedroom on the second floor. It too was full of boxes that were yet to be unpacked along with a bed that only had sheet and a couple of pillows on it. Just as he was about to go search in another room, his girlfriend Margret stepped out of the adjoining bathroom with an empty box in hand. When she made eye-contact with him, she stopped.

"Boy, you were down there a while," she remarked with a smirk, "Did you get it open?"

"Nah," Jeremy replied, "I tried everything to get that stupid safe open but nothing's working. It's like that thing was made out adamantium or something!"

"Why not call a locksmith?"

"Nuh-uh, this is a matter of pride now! I'm going to get that thing open even if I have to rent a jackhammer to do it."

Margret snickered.

"Alright, handyman," she teased, "By the way, I'm getting hungry. Can you go pick up some food for us?"

"Yeah," Jeremy sighed, realizing he could use a break, "I spotted a Wendy's not far from here."

"Ooooo! A Frosty sounds really good right now."

"Okay. The usual?"

"Yup."

"Alright, I'll be back in a few."

"Don't forget the napkins!"

He winked at her then went back down the stairs. Grabbing his keys and wallet, he strolled out the front door of his new home to the waiting truck in the driveway. As soon as he pulled onto the road, he realized he forgot his phone but mentally waved that thought away. It was only going to be about a twenty minutes trip. After a few wrong turns and navigating an absurdly complicated parking lot, he finally got in line for the Wendy's drive through. As he tapped his fingers to the music playing on the radio, his thoughts returned to the safe. From what they were told, the house was old, but it had only been on the market for a couple of months and the real estate agent never mentioned a mysterious safe in the basement.

Who put it there in the first place? Why was there no mention of it from anyone? Why wouldn't the previous owners take it with them? What is inside?

Before he could theorize further, someone behind him honked their horn and he realize the line had moved. He waved and pulled forward to put in his order. Soon he was on his way back home with a couple bags of fast food in the passenger seat. When he pulled into his driveway, he noticed that the light in the attic was on. He gathered up the food and rushed to the door but when he stepped inside, he found that the house was quiet. There wasn't even any music accompanied by Margret's singing. It was also extremely cold, like he had just stepped inside a freezer. He shrugged it off to put the food on the kitchen counter.

"Margret! I'm back!" He called.

No answer. Not even a sarcastic "nobody's home".

"Margret? Can you hear me? Do you need help up there?"

He was about to go up the stairs when he saw his phone on top of a box in the hallway. When he picked it up, there were several messages from her.

[Hey, don't forget to ask for no pickles on my burger.]

"I wasn't going to forget," he muttered to himself.

[Also, I'm going to put some of your old photography stuff in the attic to get it out of the way for now.]

[Man, it's super creepy up here.]

[I think we need to put some insulation in here before winter.]

[Um, was this box up here before?]

[Holy shit! Look what I found!]

      Below that message was a series of pictures. The first was of a small wooden box tucked in a corner. Next was a close-up of the opened box with a note inside. Last was the note unfolded, revealing a short message written in cursive.

      "We know you will find the safe in the basement. Whatever you do, do not open it! Not until you are able to find someone with enough power and knowledge to guide you through the process. It took everything we had to seal it away. Below is the combination for when you find help but please do not open it until you are prepared to fight it!"

      At the bottom of the page were three numbers: the code.

[Ha ha! Two hours for nothing!]

[Who leaves a combination for a safe you don't want anyone opening?]

[Hello? Are you getting these?]

[Hello?????]

[Oh well. I'm going to go open it myself! You better answer before I change my mind~]

[I'm going down the stairs.]

[I'm in the kitchen.]

[I am at the basement door right now~]

[You better say something to stop me~]

[Did you forget your phone again?]

[Oh well, I guess I'll have to open it myself~]

[Last chance~]

      The last message was a picture of the safe in the basement, still closed, with Margret's hand on the knob. A sinking dread overcame Jeremy. He ran to the basement door and looked down. Instead of the twilight sun streaming in from the small side window, it was pitch-black.

      "Margret!" He called out.

No response. He turned on his phone's flashlight and barreled down the steps. When he got to the bottom, he shone the light over to the safe and saw all his tools were gone. The only thing on the ground was Margret's phone and the safe was now cracked open. Anxiety flooded Jeremy's head as he knelt by the hunk of metal. He placed a hand on the door, took a deep breath, and pulled it open.

Empty.

The safe was empty and pristine as if no time passed. Jeremy stared in confusion until he felt a hand plop on his shoulder. He screeched like a little girl, dropping his phone in the process. But the minute he recognized Margret's sparkly blue nail polish, he relaxed.

"Jesus Christ, you scared the shit out of me!" He gasped.

He grabbed onto her hand but found that it was limp. He looked up to see that the arm ended in a bloody stump at the elbow and was held by a boney, grey hand.

Chatting in the Attic

It was the dead of night, but she looked both ways when she got to the road anyways. She read too many articles of hit-and-runs to even think of crossing without looking. After she ran to the other side, she continued down the sidewalk before turning into an alley. She passed the dumpster to get to a lowered fire escape ladder attached to the abandoned apartment building. Her grandpa told her it was constructed in the 1920s and she believed him. The architecture was old-fashioned but charming. Had it been maintained; it would have been the hottest place for hipsters to call home. But now, it stood alone without any renovations for fifty years. It's the type of place that urban explorers would frequent, or homeless people would squat in.

They didn't though, and she knew why.

She reached into her gym bag to pull out a pair of gardening gloves. After putting them on and scrunching her fingers, she started to climb the rusty ladder. With each rung climbed, her anxiety grew. She never liked heights; she was always too afraid to fall. However, she kept her eyes up as she reached the first story, then crawled into the open window. She had to force it open the first time she came, and it refused to go back down again. Doesn't matter, it made things easier for her in the long run.

If people thought the outside of the building was bad, they would consider the inside a B-horror movie from the 70s. From the wallpaper to the furniture left over, it was an interior designer's nightmare. She didn't mind though; she enjoyed the atmosphere. After taking in the stuffy air, she put her gloves away and pulled out a giant camping flashlight. She switched it on and started up the stairs. Each step creaked as she climbed, avoiding the broken and weak boards. She clung to the railing, carefully making her way up three stories. Along the way, she heard scurrying along the floor and within the walls. When she first visited, it terrified her. Now, she knew what it was and had accepted it.

Before long, she was standing in front of the ladder leading to the attic; the scurrying became more excited as she climbed it. Unlike the rest of the building, the attic was only bare wooden floors and walls with only a few ancient décor items tucked away as storage. The only things that could be considered insulation were the cobwebs and the layer of dust on the ground. Her own footprints from previous visits were the only sign of human life along with the pile of pillows she had made in the center of the room.

She took in a deep breath, then sighed. In that moment, she was calm. She knows she shouldn't be, there were many creepy stories about this place that have kept even the bravest kids away when she was younger. But the combination of the silence and the ancient, Earthy scent filled her with a sense of nostalgia. For some reason, she felt at home. She went up to the mountain of pillows, set her bag down, and crawled on top of it, facing the wall.

Once she got comfortable, she put down the flashlight, pointing straight ahead. She reached into her bag to take out a thick notebook almost three quarters full and her favorite black pen. After opening it, she stared at the blank page with a blank mind while tapping it with her pen. Then, a thought popped into her head. It was so random and so weird, yet the minute it surfaced, she started writing; taking that one strand of thought in whatever direction it was going. The more she wrote, the freer she felt. She was in Nirvana.

As she scribbled down words like a lunatic, the scurrying continued around her. Most of them kept their distance but a few brave, eight-legged souls crept closer. They were told to not go near her; they were even told to ignore her completely. No human dared to venture into their domain, but she kept returning over and over again. The elders had no idea what to think, the young were curious. She could hear them all around her, but she didn't care. They didn't bother her, and she didn't want to bother them.

She was in the middle of a sentence when she heard a soft thud, like a footstep done in fuzzy slippers. The scurrying paused; they knew who was coming. She swallowed the spit in her mouth and lifted her pen from the paper as the soft thuds drew closer. Her heart raced but she kept calm; it was only a matter of time before this happened. She knew the rumors, but she didn't know how this would end. Regardless, she set her pen aside as two giant tarantula legs came down in front of her.

"What are you doing here?" A booming voice demanded.

The resonance of those words sent a shiver up her spine, but she stayed calm. Without turning to face what was behind her, she straightened up and cleared her throat.

"I came here to write," she explained softly.

There was nothing but ambience after her answer. Whoever stood behind her grunted while figuring out what to say next. Some of the smaller spiders formed a circle around her, watching in awe.

"Why have you come here to 'write'?" They asked.

"I like the peace and quiet," she replied.

"There are other places you can go for that."

"I know. I just like it here."

They huffed; she bit her lip. A couple of the younger spiders approached her cautiously. They got right up to the pillow corners when the figure snarled at them, causing them to retreat behind their elders. She didn't move. The floorboards creaked as the figure leaned to hover over her. A dirty hand reached out from behind her, going for her notebook. She pulled away out of instinct, the sudden movement scattering the onlookers. The hand froze mid-air for a few seconds before retracting.

"What's wrong?" They asked.

"It's just- I don't normally share what I write with others," she explained.

"I would like to see it."

"They're just random ideas I jotted down. They're not much."

"I'd like to see for myself."

She clutched the notebook tightly once more before holding it out. The hand took it and the figure shifted back to their original position. For a little while, the only sound in the room was flipping pages. She sat nervously, staring into one of the corners of the room as her breath quickened.

"'What mysteries lay inside those petals

That dance with the flow of the autumn wind

Locked away from prying eyes and admirers

Refusing to be seen in the light of day

Only under the darkness of night do they open up

Enlightening the world with the knowledge they withhold'"

With each word read, she turned a darker shade of pink. She hunched over in shame, waiting for whatever criticism to come. Instead, her notebook reappeared in front of her.

"Did you write this here?" They asked.

"Um, no. I wrote that one in a coffee shop between classes," she replied.

"Hm."

The notebook disappeared again, and she returned to staring at the corner. There was more page turning with the occasional grunt from the reader. As time passed, the spiders approached her again. A few finally managed to crawl onto the pillows and into her lap. She opened her hand to let them explore her fingers. Then the notebook was lowered down to her again, turned back to the page she was working on. She reached out to take it and the hand pulled away.

"You've written a lot," they commented.

"Yeah," she said shyly, "I hope to get published one day."

"I'm sure you will."

The two legs stepped back and she heard the figure crawl towards the attic ladder.

"You may come here whenever you wish so long as you respect our home," they told her, "If you deface this building in any way, you will be punished."

She glanced over her shoulder to get a glimpse of the speaker. They were mostly out of the room, but she did catch the very tattered edges of a bedsheet repurposed as a cloak covering four tarantula legs.

"Will I be seeing you around?" She asked.

The figure stopped.

"Perhaps," they replied.

"I don't mind the company. I can bring my other journals for you to read as well."

"I'll...consider it," the figure replied as they pulled their other legs through, "I must attend to some matters. Enjoy your night."

Its steps traveled down the hall until she could no longer hear them. The spiders finally crawled off of her to go about their business. Some remained but most dispersed to other parts of the room. She shifted in her seat then looked back at her notebook. On the top of the page was a smudge from when it was held. She winced a bit but chose to ignore it. After re-reading what she wrote, she picked up where she left off, scribbling furiously under the glow of her flashlight.

Tar

Eighties rock blared through the speakers of the small bar. There were only a dozen patrons inside, all doing their own thing. Some played pool while their girlfriends watched, others sat at the bar, staring into their drinks. Among these people, Mark gazed at the rim of his empty glass. His brown eyes traced the top, afraid that if he stopped, he might fade away. In his mind, the voices of the day kept replaying, pecking at his skull.

"I don't want any of your excuses. Get to work!"

"Why can't you do anything right?!"

"You'll have to pick up your car on Monday, sir."

"I'm sorry.... I just can't do this anymore."

Mark groaned as more voices filled his head. When the bartender passed by, he waved him down.

"Can I get another one?" He begged, fumbling to get his wallet out.

"I think you've had enough," the bartender said.

"One more and I'll be on my way."

"Sir, I can't do that."

"Please! Just one more!"

The bartender signaled to the bouncer, who came over to grab Mark by the coat.

"Hey! Let me go!" He cried as he was dragged towards the front door.

The bouncer ignored his pleas and tossed him out of the building. Mark barely managed to land on his feet and almost ran into a group. He looked back at the door where the bouncer stood glaring at him. People walked around him as if he were a traffic cone. He hung his head in shame and stumbled down the sidewalk, attempting to blend in. The voices in his head returned, making him even more miserable. He ducked into an alley to avoid being seen but in its darkness, the voices grew louder, ripping their way into his mind.

"Shut up!" He hissed, "Leave me alone!"

Halfway through the alley, he got the feeling that he was being followed. He sped up to put distance between whoever was behind him. However, once he heard the clacking of high heels, he stopped. He glanced back to see a woman walking towards him. As she drew closer, he could make out some of her features. Long black hair that cascaded perfectly over her shoulders and a curvy body snuggly wrapped in a black dress with a slit down the side, exposing her thigh. Mark watched in awe as she stopped right in front of him with a coy smile. His eyes traced her figure hungrily until she reached out to stroke his cheek.

"You look awful," she cooed, "Rough day?"

Mark opened his mouth to answer but he couldn't find the words. She chuckled then leaned in.

"I can make your troubles go away," she whispered, "All you have to do is come with me."

She wrapped her arms around his neck and pulled herself closer. Mark didn't make a sound, he only stared at her lustfully. Then he nodded his head excitedly. The woman's smile grew, and she leaned in to kiss him on the lips. At contact, he immediately felt nauseous. His brain started spinning as if he were on a carnival ride. Before he could comprehend what was going on, his vision went black.

. . .

"Mark~. Wake up~."

Mark opened his eyes a little. The woman was sitting next to him now, but he felt like a ragdoll propped against a wall. He tried to sit up, but it was as if his limbs were filled with cement. Panicked, he looked over to the woman who was still giving him a serpent-like grin. She stroked his hair a few times before standing up to walk away. He looked around to find himself inside an abandoned warehouse surrounded by other men laying close by, still breathing but unable to move. He struggled again to get up but failed.

"Don't fight it. You'll hurt yourself," the woman said over her shoulder, "Besides, you're going to be here for a very long time. You might as well get used to it."

As she strolled away, Mark noticed her dress was moving with the consistency of oil strands coming out, attaching themselves to the other men like leeches. He looked down to his leg where a similar strand wrapped around his ankle, pumping her essence into him while draining his energy. He barely managed to drop his jaw to let out a defeated whimper.

The Horror Muse

It was 10:34 pm. Jacob knew this because he had glanced at his alarm clock six minutes ago to check if any time had passed. He wanted to groan but didn't bother. The only ones who would hear were himself and maybe his basset hound, Red, who was sleeping on the bed. From the corner of his eye, Jacob watched the dog doze on the messy sheets that hadn't been washed in months, envying his care-free rest. His eyes then drifted over to his bunched-up work uniform in the corner and he grimaced.

He looked back at the clock. 10:38. He glanced out the window to look at the parking lot below. Golden-orange streets lamps illuminated the area, giving off a "behind the bar dumpster" vibe. One of them was flickering just above where he had parked. In the apartment complex across the street, he could see some of the lights still on with people watching television or finishing the last of their daily chores before bed. Most were dark. Jacob took another look at the clock. 10:41.

How could time be this slow?

With a sigh, he brought his attention back to the open Word document with nothing in it. The text cursor blinked at the top left corner mockingly, daring him to try something. He glared back at it in disgust. Every time he tried to type something, it would immediately be deleted for several reasons. Too cliché. Too boring. Too over-the-top. No matter what he tried it always came out wrong and that damned cursor would always be there, laughing at his failures. Too many times he wanted to throw his computer out the window but he couldn't afford a replacement. And the landlord would be pissed at him for breaking the window.

A gnat buzzed by his face, almost smacking him in the forehead. He tried to swat it but missed. It zoomed towards the empty dinner plate where a small swarm of bugs slurped up the remaining pizza roll grease while others circled around the tip of a lukewarm beer. Jacob waved his hand above the plate to scatter them then grabbed the beer before they could reclaim it. He downed what little was left and tossed it into the trash with the gnats followed. Once enough of them were gathered, he pulled the trash bag strings to trap them inside and sat back in his chair with a small bit of satisfaction. The cursor continued to blink at him. He glanced at the clock: 10:47. With a grunt, he stood up from his desk. Red poked his head up as his human stretched his back. Jacob noticed and gave him a good scratch behind the ears.

"Come on Red, let's get you a treat," he said.

The dog's tail thumped on the bed in excitement. Jacob smirked. He picked up the plate and pulled the very full trash bag out of the bin before shuffling out of the bedroom. Red hopped down to follow. Both of them strode into the kitchen that hadn't been cleaned in ages. Dishes piled up in the sink, crumbs were all over the counter, and plastic wrappers littered the floor. Jacob stopped to analyze the mess; the disgustingness finally hitting him in the face. Red waddled up right next to his human's leg. After a few moments of them standing in silence, he placed a paw on Jacob's calf, scratching it softly.

"Nnn?" Jacob finally snapped back to reality, "Oh, right. Hang on there, buddy."

He put the trash bag by the front door and dish in the sink then reached up to grab a box on top of the refrigerator. Red immediately sat down to look patient but his tail wagged eagerly. Jacob laughed as he pulled out a small brown biscuit.

"Can you sit up?" He asked.

Red hoisted himself up on his hind legs with his front paws out in front of him; his small beady eyes opened wide. He reminded Jacob of Oliver.

"Okay boy, here you go." He said as he tossed the treat to the ground.

Red dropped the innocent act to devour the biscuit while Jacob put the box back on top of the refrigerator. He turned to go back to his bedroom but stopped when he saw the white glow on his door. The stupid cursor was waiting for him, waiting for his next failure. His attention went back to the ant infested kitchen.

Meh. It can wait. I've been pushing this back for too long.

After some pondering over where to start, he began gathering the trash scattered on the floor and counter. Then he wiped down the countertops and scrubbed the dishes, all while bobbing his head to some eight-bit video game music he heard from work. Soon the bachelor's kitchen was clean; or as clean as a wet paper towel could get it. With the job done, Jacob stood back to admire his handywork.

His pride was quickly dissipated by the remembrance of the blank terror in the other room. Off to the side he saw Red slumped on the couch, staring at him tiredly. Jacob walked over and plopped down next to him. Red shifted his position so that his head draped over his human's lap while Jacob began to scratch his ears. For a while they sat in their peaceful bubble of bliss in the night.

Jacob felt his eyelids begin to droop and shook the sleepiness away, looking around for something to occupy his mind. He glanced at a few stacks of books on his coffee table gathering dust: his collection. There was the King stack containing *Needful Things*, *IT*, and *Pet Sematary*. To the right were the classics: *Frankenstein*, *Dracula*, and *The Complete Works of H.P. Lovecraft*. Then there were the random piles with titles ranging from *Stardust* to *The Hellbound Heart*. There used to be more, but he sold them to pay for groceries and beer.

At the very corner of the table, he saw a beaten-up hardcover book the size of a bible. He carefully lifted his hand from Red's furry head and reached over to grab it. *The Complete Works of Edgar Allan Poe*; the gospel of his angsty teenage years. He held the behemoth collection into both hands, just staring at the cover. It was a used copy he found at the thrift store and impulsively bought to relive both fond and embarrassing memories. His fingers brush the spine as his eyes traced the author's name over and over again.

Maybe if I whack myself in the face with this enough times, the genius will spill into my brain and I'll come up with something.

A tempting idea, but the thought of dealing with the resulting headache was enough to keep him from falling through with that plan. Instead, he continued to hold the book, hoping to absorb the inspiration through osmosis if he stared at it long enough. Several moments passed before he looked over to the kitchen stove for the time. 11:27. Finally, he let out a deep sigh.

Alright. Let's get this stupid ball rolling.

He wiggled his leg to wake Red then got up. After making a short detour to the refrigerator, he planted his rear in the desk chair and opened one of the two beers he grabbed. He took a sip then got his hands into position on the keyboard. It took about ten minutes of thinking before his fingers started typing.

"The moon was full as Jenny walked through the-"

The cursor stopped moving as Jacob stared at the nine words in front of him. He repeated them over and over in a soft whisper until they became poison to his tongue. On the sixth reread, he slammed his index finger on the backspace key. He could almost hear the cursor cackling at him as it backed up. If it had a neck, he would wring it. He sipped his beer while plotting his next attempt when a knock came at his front door, nearly making him choke. Jacob looked over to Red laying on the bed who was just as confused. No other sound came. He shrugged.

"Must have the wrong address," he muttered to himself.

Red lay his head back down but kept eyeing the doorframe. Jacob forced a smile and scratched his ear.

"It's okay buddy. It's probably some drunk idiot," he cooed.

Turning back to his blank computer screen, the feeling of dread came back. He downed the rest of the beer and cracked open the next one. Just as he threw the empty bottle in the trash, another knock came. This time it was firmer and sharper. Now Jacob was starting to get nervous. Red sat up on the bed, eyes fixed on the door. They both waited until knocking came again, even louder than before. Red started to growl while Jacob rolled his eyes.

They're not going to leave, are they?

He stood up and stormed out of the room with Red chasing after him. Soon, the two of them were at the door. Red growled in a menacing tone, pulling back his lips to show his teeth. Jacob felt his heart pound in his chest. He went to turn the lock but stopped when he noticed all the hairs on his forearm were standing up. His fingers shook while a chill ran through his body.

What the hell? What's going on?

Another knock came and Red barked. Jacob stooped down to calm him, but he refused to stand down. He was not going to be polite to whomever was on the other side. Once Jacob finally got him to sit semi-quietly, he turned back to the door. With a final glance to Red, he twisted the knob and flung it wide open. No one was there. The only thing that greeted him was the apartment right across from him, all shut up for the night. Jacob looked out and down the hall for any trace of life then pulled the door closed.

A prank? But.... why? And why this late on a Thursday night?

Then he realized that Red had stopped growling. He looked down at his side, but the dog was gone. Panicked, he went to open the door again when he heard heavy panting. He whirled around and his heart stopped. Red had somehow made it all the way over to the couch and was now staring at a figure cloaked in black. The thing extended a sickly pale hand out which he sniffed vigorously before licking it. The hand migrated to his floppy ears and gave them a scratch. Red opened his mouth in a dopey smile, his tail wagging excitedly. Jacob backed up against the kitchen counter. All the "who", "what", and "whys" going through his head were only met with more questions. Slowly, he crept his way along the wall so not to startle his "guest".

Once he got to the opposite side of the room, he could see its cracked fingernails and a faint greyish-green discoloration on some parts of its skin. His gaze followed up the slender arm, noticing that the figure was wearing a tattered and loose fitting black peplos. Still, he could make out the voluptuous feminine frame underneath. Finally, Jacob's eyes reached the face. She was almost gorgeous. If it weren't for the spots of mold-like discoloration and the deep violet shadows around her eyes, she would have looked like a finely sculpted statue. Even her black lips and long dark hair that contrasted with her pale skin added to her ethereal aura. She was a ghastly beauty; a captivating ghoul that was now sitting in his living room petting his clueless dog.

Jacob's eyes went back and forth between her and the door, baffled as to how she slipped past him. Then he looked down at Red, who was apparently now fine with the lovely zombie that was scaring them earlier. Questions kept whirling in his head, but he shook them away to focus on what to do next. He slowly knelt down and extended his hand out.

"Come here Red," he whispered urgently.

The woman lifted her head up to look at him, turning his blood to ice. Her eyes were bright yellow with small black dots in the center; not at all what he expected. They stared into his very being, analyzing his soul. He tried to ignore them and return his attention to his dog.

"Red. Come here!" He ordered.

Red looked back at him, confused as to why his human was hostile. The woman's hand continued to rub his body, but his tail had stopped wagging. Out of frustration, Jacob snapped his fingers which finally got the dog to waddle over to him. He pulled Red close to examine him, praying that the mold hadn't spread onto him. To his relief, there was nothing. He looked back up at the woman sitting on his couch, her face completely devoid of emotion. Jacob released Red then nudged him with his arm.

"Go to my room Red," he whispered.

Red tilted his head but did as he was told, trotting to the bedroom as fast as he could. With that taken care of, Jacob stood up and puffed out his chest.

"Who are you?" He demanded, trying to sound tough.

The woman just looked him up and down. Wherever her gaze landed, it felt like something was crawling under his skin.

"I said, who are you? Answer me!" He demanded, "What are you doing in my apartment?"

She raised an eyebrow, unimpressed, then turned her focus towards the stacks of books on the table. When she reached out to the Poe collection, Jacob stepped forward to smack her hand away.

"Don't touch that!" He barked.

The woman snapped her head up to glare at him, making him instantly shrink away. He stood down as she turned back to the book, picking it up. Minutes passed as she thumbed through the pages without a word. Jacob could feel his resolve evaporating. Before he let it disappear completely, he tried once again to puff out his chest.

"Get out! Now!"

At this order, the woman looked up, eyes narrowed.

"Get out or I'm calling the cops!"

Suddenly, she stood up, looking irate. At that moment, Jacob remembered that his phone was back in his bedroom. She took a step forward and he immediately backed into the wall with a slight fear that he might lose his bowels. Every ounce of bravery in him was gone. She furrowed her brow then briskly walked past him towards his bedroom. All he could do was stare ahead at the poster for *Army of Darkness* on the opposite wall as he slid down to the floor. He was brought back to Earth by a tongue lapping at his fingers. Red had returned to him, looking concerned. Jacob patted his head gently then got back on his feet and trudged over to the bedroom with Red following.

The woman was sitting at his computer desk when he entered, staring at the screen. Her cloak was now strewn on the bed, leaving her shoulders exposed. Red hopped up on the bed as he always did and made himself comfortable. The woman noticed and gave him a pat as he closed his eyes for another nap. She then turned to face Jacob and motioned to the blank computer screen while her expression morphed into disappointment.

"You're here for my story?" He asked.

She kept staring while he squirmed in his place.

"Don't look at me like that," he pleaded, "I have ideas but I just can't put them down on the page. Every time I have something, I lose it once I get home from work."

His gaze dropped to the floor; even he could hear how pathetic he sounded. When he lifted his head back up the woman's face had softened. She looked down at the book on her lap and stoked it again, slowing at the author's name. For some reason, this made a little bubble of anger come up from his gut.

"Oh, come on! He wasn't any different from me! He was a freaking drunk for most of his life and a depressed mess!"

The woman shot him a glare that forced him to step back, bumping his shoulder on the doorframe. Eventually her face relaxed but her annoyance stayed. His eyes fell again.

"I'm sorry. It's just- I used to be so much better at this. Getting stuff down, not the actual writing. I was shit back then but, it didn't matter. I loved doing it and I kept getting better. But then school happened, then work and I just...lost my spark. I tried to get it back; I read the greats, watched advice videos, went to the classes. But...I just can't get my inspiration back."

He looked up to see woman leaning back in the chair.

"Aren't you going to say anything?" He demanded.

To this question, a wide grin broke on her face, and she beckoned for him to come closer. Jacob hesitated but slowly crept over. Once he was close enough, she opened her mouth. In the glow of the computer light, he could see that beyond her grey teeth was a black, fleshy stump where a tongue used to be. He recoiled in disgust while she chuckled.

"This is too weird."

Then he felt a cold hand slither onto his hip. He yelped as he jumped forward and spun around. The woman smirked before setting the book on the desk and standing up. Suddenly, the door to his bedroom slammed shut. He rushed over to open it but no matter how hard he pulled or pushed, it wouldn't budge. Again, he felt a clammy hand, this time on his shoulder. He turned to see that the woman was only inches from his face. Jacob pressed his body against the door, hoping he'd squeeze through the wood to escape.

The woman continued to smile as she pulled herself closer. Her ghostly arms wrapped around his neck while her hips pressed against him; she was surprisingly soft despite how cold her skin was. Out of reflex, his hands moved to grab her by the waist. She smirked again then stood up on her toes. Before he could react, her dark lips pressed onto his mouth. A low moan came from her throat that immediately intoxicated him. The room began to spin until everything went black. For a long while, nothing happened as he floated in the void. He tried to feel around for something to grab onto but found nothing. He opened his mouth to shout but was mute. It was as if he was in a dimension of emptiness. All he could do was float around and try not to cry.

The silence was abruptly broken by a loud clap of thunder. He stiffened to attention and found himself in a long hallway with purple wallpaper and black wooden floors. There were dozens of black doors on each side leading up to a tall, thin window at the end of the hall. Above him, he could hear heavy raindrops pounding on the roof. A flash of lightning crackled its way across the night sky, lighting up the corridor, followed by booming rumble.

From that brief moment of light, he saw one door was slightly ajar as if begging for him to approach. Every bone in his body shivered at the idea of going anywhere near it; especially since he was still unsure of how he even got there. Nonetheless, he shifted his weight to sneak towards it. The moment his foot hit the floor, the wood creaked loudly, echoing throughout the space. Just under the sound of the rain, he heard a shuffle from somewhere.

"Shit!" He whispered.

He desperately wanted to run but with no idea where to go or what would happen next, there was no other option but to keep going. Each step he took resulted in a loud groan from the floorboards no matter how hard he tried to be quiet. As he came closer, a faint scratching sound started up between the claps of thunder. They were long, slow and far too intentional to be written off as rats. Something was biding its time until he got there.

Finally, he reached the door and there was no doubt the scratching sounds were coming from within the dark room. His stomach twisted itself up as he gently pushed the wood. It swung open from the small force, further adding to his anxiety. He waited for another flash of lightning to scan the room. The few white cracks gave him just enough time to see a large wooden desk by the window, a bookcase stretching around the room, and two large leather chairs facing the desk.

Still uneasy, he took a step inside. Something sharp stabbed the bottom of his foot, making him cry out in pain and fall back. He looked down to see a clear shard of glass sticking out of his skin. Blood was oozing out of the site, dripping onto the hardwood floor. Jacob bit his lip while grabbing the shard to give it a tug. The sensation of his skin following the pull made him nauseous. It took a few tries for it to come out smoothly and he held back the urge to vomit while he checked for more pieces.

As he examined the damage, he noticed that the scratching had stopped. Another flash of lightning illuminated the room and he saw a shattered water glass on the floor just past the doorway. Several other knickknacks were strewn about haphazardly. He noticed the indents in the rug where the chair was moved and a splatter of red on the carpet. The scratching suddenly started back up again, nearly giving him a heart attack. It was coming from behind the desk, right underneath the windowsill. Jacob spotted someone collapsed close by, motionless. A spark of courage put him to action, and he slowly crawled over to them, maneuvering around the shattered glass the best he could. The scratching continued on; it knew he was there.

He stopped in front of the desk to put a barrier between him and the noise, taking the time to catch his breath. Then he peered around to see the body was a man in a suit. Another crackle of light flashed that showed his eyes frozen in terror. His face was deathly white except for four bright red claw marks running down his face. Jacob ducked back behind the desk, stifling a scream. At that moment, there was one long, deep scratch that pierced his ears. It was getting impatient. Jacob glanced around for something to defend himself with. After a lightening flash, he saw a hole puncher underneath one of the leather chairs and scurried over to grab it. Then he stood up, despite the pain in his foot, taking a final deep breath before stepping around the desk.

The first thing he saw was the head of a person crouched behind the office chair. They had long greasy black hair that hung over their shoulders and wore a hospital gown to cover their emaciated body. Jacob squinted to see its arms moving up and down in time with the scratches. More lightning showed long, thin talons in place of fingers digging into the wall like knives. A gasp escaped Jacob's throat and they stopped moving. It sat still for a moment before turning to face him. He gripped the hole puncher tightly.

"Don't even think about it," he hissed.

The figure pulled their talons away from the wall and stood up. They met him in height, but their gangly frame made them look taller. A flash of light revealed their grey, glassy eyes staring through him, but Jacob's attention fell to the lower half of the face. Instead of a jaw, there was a gapping red hole exposing their throat. By the way the skin was shredded, it looked like it had been torn out. The gory sight shocked Jacob into dropping the hole puncher. The figure stared at him while a gurgle came from its exposed esophagus. Then they raised their hand and clicked their talons together.

Jacob sprinted for the door while the figure gave chase. They swiped for him but missed by an inch and growled in frustration. Jacob jumped over the broken glass and back into the hallway. His eyes zoomed in on the door across the way and he reached for it, bursting his way in then slamming the door shut and locked it. There was a loud thud from the figure running into the wood followed by a frustrated scream. They scratched and banged on the door, but the barrier was too strong. Realizing defeat, they threw one last hit before scurrying away. Finally feeling safe in the darkness, Jacob slid down to the ground and pulled his knees to his chest.

He sat there for a long time while his heart pounded like crazy. Once his breathing returned to normal, he lifted his head to figure out where he was. The floor felt like concrete beneath his feet while the low rumblings of a water heater came from one direction and the swishing of a washing machine came from another. Then a dim yellow outline of a door appeared high above him. The glow was bright enough for him to see totes of holiday decorations nearby, white plastic piping along the wall, and wooden steps going up to the doorframe.

Basement?

Jacob felt behind him for the door, but it was gone; instead replaced by a cinderblock wall. The sounds of thunder and rain were gone but the gash in his foot remained. Now he was really confused. Using the wall, he pulled himself up and hobbled to the bottom of the stairs. He climbed about halfway up before the bloodcurdling scream of a young girl stopped him. Then he heard a middle-aged woman start shouting and the two went back and forth until he heard a loud slap. A door was opened and the screeching of something metal being dragged grated on his ears.

"Get in there! Both of you!" The woman screamed.

The girl tried to protest and a third voice from a boy piped up. Another slap echoed down the steps and Jacob heard the girl begin to cry. They shuffled to a different part of the room then there was the loud creaking of a cage door.

"Get in!" The woman commanded.

Now the boy was crying along with the girl.

"Mom, please stop," he begged.

Slap

More shuffling followed. The cage door slammed shut, followed by the rattling of a chain wrapping around it. The woman stormed off while the teens muttered to each other. Jacob gripped the railing, wondering if he had time to run in and free them. His hopes were dashed when the thumping footsteps of the woman carrying something heavy came back. The teens screamed in terror.

"What are those things?!" The girl shrieked.

"Shut up, you whore!" The woman shot back.

"Mom! Please don't do this!" The boy pleaded.

"Shut up!"

Jacob heard a large plastic container open followed by little scuttles and chirps. The teens pleaded one last time then shrieked as the scuttling became more frantic. Eventually, the container was tossed aside, and the woman stormed off. The teens screamed in agony while a television was turned on. Something small scurried toward the doorframe only to bump into the wood and hurry away. A feeling of dread flooded over Jacob as he realized that his only way out was through that door. He slowly climbed up to the last step, grabbed the doorknob, and pushed it open.

The color yellow assaulted his vision while the ceiling light nearly blinded him. There were dirty yellow tiles, yellow floral curtains on the window above the sink, yellow everything. Once his eyes adjusted, a red spot on the floor caught his eye. It was a beetle-like creature but more nightmarish. Its back looked like red plated armor with a stinger on its backside and large, sharp pincers on its front. Its tiny black eyes locked onto him for a moment before charging. Jacob spotted a baseball bat leaning next to the basement door and grabbed it without hesitation, swinging down for a direct hit. The beetle's innards splattered all over the lemon tiles.

He stepped over the dead insect and turned right. Just outside the open kitchen on the other side of the dining room table, he saw a dog kennel maybe big enough for a greyhound. Inside were the two teens frantically squirming around naked, while hundreds of red beetles crawled over them, biting and stinging wherever they could. The girl was trying to stand up to get away while the boy kicked the cage door. Their blood dripped everywhere, making their small enclosure slippery. A purple sequined dress with matching heels and a black suit were bunched up on the floor close by.

Beyond the horror show was the glow of a television playing a wrestling match. In a sofa chair parked right in front of it was the woman, mindlessly watching. She held a can of beer and on the side table next to her was a pistol. Jacob looked back at the couple, now coated in a thin layer of blood. They continued to fight against the cage as the beetles crawled across every crease and cranny of their bodies. The boy looked over to the sofa chair in desperation.

"Why are you doing this?" He cried.

The woman slowly pulled her gaze from the television to stare at them. There was nothing in her eyes

"Because I can," she grunted before turning away.

The boy lost his grip and landed on the bottom of the cage, weeping. A flurry of beetles piled onto him as the girl continued to beat on the cage door. In her frenzy, she spotted Jacob.

"Help us! Please!" She begged.

Jacob couldn't move; he thought the action in his head, but his body refused to do anything. Then he felt a sharp jab on his shin and looked down. One of the beetles had buried its pincers into his flesh. He quickly smacked in onto the floor and stomped on it, splattering it like the first one. The back armor stabbed into his already cut skin. More beetles took notice and charged for him with clicking pincers at the ready and he ran for the basement door, dropping the bat as he went. When the floor dipped under him, he realized his mistake. All he could do was bring his arms up to protect his face.

The fall was much longer and more brutal than he expected with all the steps he tumbled down. He only felt relief when he landed face first onto the ground. It took him a few minutes of lying motionless to realize that he had landed on grass, not concrete. When the scent of rotting wood and fallen leaves reached his nostrils, he lifted his head to see that he was now in the middle of a forest in the middle of night. A wave of relief washed over him as he sat up, thankful that the hell he came from was gone.

As he rubbed his aching back, he spotted a sliver of light between the trees off in the distance. He scrambled to his feet to run towards it; wherever it was had to be better than the dark unknown. When he broke the forest line, he was shocked to find it was an old cottage with a candle lantern hanging next to the door. There was more light inside so Jacob ran towards it without any more questions. After busting his way in, he quickly shut the door then leaned on it to catch his breath. He looked around and noticed that all the furniture and decor was colonial style. From the plain wood table sandwiched between two benches, to the basin and washboard in the corner, to the real burning fireplace. It was as if he had fallen back in time.

"Historical recreation?" He guessed.

Then he saw a ladder in the corner leading up to the second floor. He was about to call out to whoever was home when he saw a giant web attached underneath its rungs with a large black spider sitting in the center. Its size made Jacob shrink away. Then he spotted another web on the wall with a white spider hovering over its kill. Anxiety nearly suffocated him as he slowly looked around to see all kinds of spiders strung up in every nook and cranny of the cottage. Above the fireplace, settled in the window, burrowed in the firewood. Some of them crawled past him as if he wasn't there, almost making him yelp.

That's when he began to hear the whispers, tiny whispers. It didn't take long for him to realize that they were coming from the arachnid horde and most of them were about him. Some of the larger spiders began to descend from their webs to come towards him. Jacob looked back at the door but found a brown spider with thin legs blocking it. He shuffled to the middle of the room as even the smaller ones were coming after him.

"Are you all right sir?"

Jacob screamed loudly and spun around to see a little albino girl in a nightgown looking just as surprised to see him as he was to see her. The contrast of her pale complexion to the Earthy cottage made her look like a ghost. He stuck out a finger to poke her; it hit cloth then a solid human shoulder. He pulled his hand away, both reassured and embarrassed while the girl gave him a confused look.

"Sir, are you alright?" She asked again.

"Er...Well, I think I am now," he responded.

"Where did you come from? Are you a villager?"

"I don't know, to be honest. I was somewhere then I ended up here."

He tried to smile while keeping an eye on the needle-legged creatures around him.

"They won't harm you," the girl assured.

"Oh. Is that so?" He croaked.

"We haven't had visitors here for a long time so they're probably just curious."

"R-right."

A grey spider dropped down from the ceiling to perch on her shoulder then crawled to her ear. Jacob heard tiny whispers but couldn't tell what it was saying. Then the girl looked down at his shin.

"You're hurt!" She gasped.

"Oh, yeah. It's a weird story."

She examined the wound for a second then pointed towards one of the benches by the table.

"Sit there," she instructed.

Before he could say anything, she rushed over to a desk he hadn't noticed before that was covered with herbs. After flipping through some books and loose papers, she set to work mixing various things together. Jacob inched towards the bench, taking care not to step on anything and ignoring the five spiders on the table. He sat on edge, focusing on the warmth of the fire while the whispering continued around him. After thoroughly crushing up some herbs, the girl went over to the fireplace where a small pot was hanging on a hook. She poured everything into it, went to the basin for water, then put it in a contraption that held it over the crackling flames. He watched her awkwardly, trying to think of something to say.

"Um, my name is Jacob."

"My name's Elisa," the girl replied, keeping her attention on the pot.

"So.... are you the only one who lives here?"

"My mother is away now. She went to visit my aunt the next village over."

"She left you here alone?"

"I'm not alone. I have them." Elisa gestured to the spiders.

"I.... see."

The cup started to bubble with some of the contents spilling onto the flames. She took a pair of tongs to pull it out then carefully walked over to the table, trying not to spill anything.

"What are you two doing all the way out here?" Jacob asked.

"Mother makes medicine," Elisa explained, as she walked back to the desk, "She wants me to practice so that I can have a trade when I leave in the spring."

"Why in the spring?"

"That's when I turn thirteen. It's when all of us go out to find a mentor. I hope I can find someone who will teach me fortune telling."

"Fortune telling? Are you serious?"

"Uh-huh."

From the cluttered mess, she pulled out a small red bottle. She returned to the table and put two drops of the liquid into the concoction. Some of the spiders crawled closer to watch her work while more collected on the table. Jacob lifted his feet onto the bench to avoid them.

"Can you tell them not get close to me?" He asked her.

Elisa looked at him confused while the whispers started back up.

"Is he telling us to leave in our own home?"

"How dare he order us around!"

"We have as much of a right to be here as anyone!"

"Everyone please calm down!" Elisa pleaded.

The whispering stopped as the spiders backed off. She looked over to Jacob apologetically.

"I'm sorry. I forgot that outsiders don't like them as much as we do."

She went back to the basin to retrieve a rag then dipped it into the pot. It was sloshed around before it was pulled back up, steaming.

"Could you put your feet down? It will be easier for me," she said.

Jacob checked that nothing was underneath him before slowly bringing his feet off the bench. Once the rag was done dripping, Elisa took it and knelt to pick up his bleeding leg.

"This may sting," she warned.

She wrapped the damp cloth around his shin carefully. A slight tingling buzzed around the bite wound but the warmth of the rag felt nice. She tied up the rag to secure it then looked up at him.

"You took that well," she remarked with a smile, "Are you injured anywhere else?"

"Y-yeah. On the bottom of my foot."

He lifted his foot just enough for her to see. She nodded then returned to the basin for another rag. It was soon drenched and wrapped over his wounds. Once it too was secured, Jacob wiggled his toes to be sure they weren't uncomfortable.

"Um... thank you," he muttered.

His hand went for his wallet, but it only hit the fabric of his basketball shorts. A couple more frantic pats confirmed his fear.

"I'm sorry. I don't have any money to give you," he admitted in shame.

"That's okay. This was an easy brew, and I needed the practice."

"But I feel so guilty."

She paused to think. A spider crawled up to her ear to whisper and she nodded.

"That's right! I almost forgot about that!" She said, "Well, if you insist on returning the favor, would you mind accompanying me somewhere?"

"I guess that depends," Jacob replied, "Where do you need to go?"

"It's not too far from here. There's a certain flower I need to gather for a specific medicine. I meant to do it sooner, but I've been putting it off all day."

Jacob thought about it for a moment, but he already knew what his answer would be.

"Okay. I just need to be careful with my foot."

Elisa let out a sigh and smiled. She hurried over to a wall where two cloaks hung: a long, black one and a smaller, blue one. Jacob stood up from the bench and hobbled after her, the rag's warmth fading with each step. When he finally reached her, she held out the black cloak to him. He pulled it on while she grabbed a twig basket and lantern by the door. They were about to leave when a black spider perched itself on the top of the door, stopping Jacob in his tracks. It crawled down to his level before it spoke.

"If anything happens to her, we will devour you."

It crawled away before he could respond. A short tug on his cloak brought him back to Earth.

"Let's go," Elisa said, handing him the lantern, "I'd like to make this quick now that it's dark."

Jacob nodded then pushed the door open. Elisa hurried over to a small open path off to the side of the house and he followed as fast as he could. Soon they were trudging through the dark forest quietly. A gust of wind shook the branches above, causing some leaves to fall on their heads. The rag on Jacob's foot grew uncomfortable as it turned into a muddy mess. He wanted to stop to remove it but Elisa was moving too quickly. Finally, they reached a clearing where hundreds of little purple flowers swayed in the breeze.

"This shouldn't take long," she said, trying to sound reassuring.

She went into the center of the clearing and began picking, being extremely selective with her takings. Jacob stood by awkwardly, sometimes looking around at the trees around them. He thought he heard a snap in the bushes, but it was too faint for him to be suspicious.

"What do you need these for, again?" He asked.

"I need them to make a potion for the miller's wife," Elisa replied, not looking up from her work, "She's expecting in the winter, but her child is restless. These will help calm the baby."

"Oh. So, you and your mother run a business?"

"Something like that. But we have to be careful with who we offer our services to."

"Why's that?"

"There are some in the village who despise us for what we do. Mother says it's because they don't understand that we are here to help."

"I see."

"Usually, I gather ingredients in the daytime and work at night. I don't like being out here in the dark."

"You and me both."

She plucked a few more blossoms then stood up.

"This should be enough for what I need. Let's go back."

As she stepped towards him, they heard a loud snap beyond the clearing. Elisa whipped around to the direction of the noise while Jacob took a few steps forward. They listened closely for anything to follow but all they could hear was the wind.

"I-it's probably just a squirrel or something," Jacob guessed, "Or maybe a possum."

"You are probably right," Elisa agreed, nodding slowly, "But let us go before-"

A shadow sprung from behind a tree, charging towards her. It wasn't until Jacob saw the gleaming ax blade that he screamed. It plunged into Elisa's skull with a loud crunch, and she fell to the ground, dropping her basket. The shadow continued to hit her with the ax while Jacob backed up into a tree, watching in horror. Blood sprinkled onto the surrounding flowers like rain as it continued to chop her up. Once she was reduced to a red mess it stopped then looked over to Jacob. In the still light, he could see that the shadow was a tall man; his white shirt and brown pants now splashed in crimson.

"Were you helping this witch?" He grunted.

Jacob sputtered; the words he wanted to say balled up in his throat. Then the man took a step closer to him.

"No, wait! Please!" he cried.

The lantern fell from his grip as the man swung the ax at him. Jacob slammed his eyes shut, preparing to die, but nothing happened. The sounds and smells of the forest disappeared in an instant. He reopened his eyes, and the forest was gone. He was now standing in the pure white corridor of a hospital; the architecture looked like it was from the thirties. Suddenly, a scream came from behind him, and he turned to see a nurse running towards him. She was clutching her neck as blood spewed between her fingers. Just as she was about to speak, she collapsed in front of him with a scarlet puddle growing around her as she exhaled for the last time. Back down the hall, an overweight man in a hospital gown with a deranged stare stood with a knife in his hands. Once they locked eyes he charged.

"Oh come on!" Jacob cried.

He sprinted down the hall in the opposite direction. When he burst through a pair of double doors marked 'exit' he fell into a void of blackness. He twisted his body around to find something to grab onto while his mind buzzed with horrific nightmares. A dark castle home to a sadistic woman in red, ready to lure him into her dungeon. A family of cannibals descending onto a carriage of rich noblemen. A group of explorers running into a shapeless creature while exploring a mysterious cave. Each vision seemed too real, and so exciting.

Jacob twisted and turned until he felt a wet tongue lick his nose. In a blink, he was back on the floor of his bedroom with Red standing over him, whining. He looked up at the dog, feeling the carpet under him, then sat up. The window was still dark, and his lamp was still on. Red continued to whine until Jacob placed his hand on his head in a limp pat. He looked over to the clock on his desk. It was 3:27 in the morning.

"I have time," he whispered.

He gave Red a hug then got on the computer. It only took him a few seconds of thinking before he began to type. His fingers flew over the keyboard, producing paragraph after paragraph of text. Vivid descriptions and dialogue filled the pages as the cursor struggled to keep up. Red watched him for a bit then looked over to the bed where the woman in black lay, reading a book. She looked down at him and his little tail thumped on the ground in excitement. She smiled and patted the empty spot next to her. He jumped up for a cuddle as she continued to read. Just as Jacob finished the inner thoughts of a killer who slaughtered his wife and kids, his alarm went off. The blaring sound scared him enough to make him fall out of his chair. Once he calmed down, he looked at the clock. 7 in the morning.

"Fuck!" He hissed.

The clock continued to blare at him until he switched it off. He sat back in his chair, contemplating whether or not to call off work. While the demon on his shoulder made excellent points, the angel won out. He quickly went through the motions of his morning routine that ended with filling Red's food and water bowls. Once he felt somewhat ready to start the day, he gave Red one last scratch behind the ears then stumbled out the door. Still laying on the bed, the woman closed her book. She walked out of the bedroom to put it back on the coffee table with the others. Red waddled up to the couch to meet her as she picked out another one to pass the time for when he returned.

Movie Date

Dress shirt or polo?

Andy pondered the two options laid out on his bed, torn between them.

I'm gonna be picking her up so I should look decent. But it is just a movie night.

After some waffling, he finally picked the green polo and pulled it over his head, turning towards the mirror hanging on his door. Any creases or wrinkles were brushed away. Satisfied with his outfit, he brought his attention to the thick red mess on top of his head. He picked up a comb to do some general straightening up but the moment he stopped, the curls popped back up. He sighed in defeat, knowing this was the best it was going to get.

Before leaving his bedroom, he did one last run through the mental checklist. Face washed. Breath fresh. Fly up. Collar fixed. He tried to convince himself that he looked fine but his hair, his slight gut, and the pimple that appeared on his cheek yesterday brought his confidence down a few pegs. Despite this, he pulled on the new leather jacket he got for his birthday then headed downstairs to the kitchen. His father was leaning over the sink, scrubbing the last pot clean while his mother sat on the couch watching her show.

"I'm going out now," he announced.

"Where are you going?" His mother yelled from her seat.

"I'm going to hang out with Tom for a little bit," he replied, suppressing the nervousness in his voice. "We're going to the movies."

"Okay, have fun! Don't be out too late."

She gave him a smile before returning her attention back to the TV. Andy went over to the counter to grab the keys to the old Sentra when his father placed a drenched hand on top of them.

"Go look in the utensil drawer," he said quietly.

Perplexed, Andy walked over to the drawer by the stove and opened it. At first glance he couldn't understand why he was there. Then he spotted a twenty-dollar bill and a familiar shiny square wrapper. He looked up in a panic while his father dried his hands.

"Don't get excited," he warned, "This is just in case something happens."

He gave his son a stern look as he handed over the car keys. Andy tucked the bill and the condom in his pocket and gave him a short nod before rushing out the door. Once he was outside, Andy checked his watch. 8:23 pm. The late summer sky was still bright orange, but the cool shadows of the houses and trees already darkened the cracked road. Within minutes, he was driving out of the neighborhood towards the farmland away from town. He tried to focus on the road and the time, but his mind kept drifting back to what he had in his pocket.

After zipping down the winding roads, he finally turned into a gravel driveway that led up to a large, black mansion in the middle of the cornfields. A couple of trees tried to grow on the property, but their withered branches reached to the sky, begging for a merciful end. Andy shook all perverted thoughts from his head just as he parked in the front. From inside the mansion, he heard the wild barking of dogs he was all too familiar with as he walked up to the porch and knocked on the door. He only had to wait a moment for a pair of yellow eyes to peer at him from the closest window. The door cracked open and two dog heads burst out but were held back by a pale, boney hand.

"Hi Clover. Hi Shamrock," Andy greeted, kneeling down.

The two-headed pooch sniffed his outstretched hand then gave it a few sloppy kisses. It sat down politely while the yellow eyes continued to glare at him.

"Hello Andy," deep voice boomed in a thick accent.

"Hello Mr. Medved," Andy returned, "Is Helen ready?"

The ghoulish man turned away and shouted something in another language. A distant voice replied followed by short, rapid clacking going down the stairs and across the front room. Then a pale girl in a light blue dress stepped out onto the porch. A white cardigan sweater covered her shoulders, for modesty, while a veil covered the lower half of her face. Andy could see the pure joy and excitement in her golden eyes as she came closer. Just gazing into them warmed his heart.

"Hi Andy!" She gasped.

"Hey Helen," Andy squeaked back, "Ready?"

"Yeah, let's go!"

He was about to turn around when the collar of his polo was snatched. A long arm had emerged from the shadows that led back to Mr. Medved's frown.

"You will have her back by 11 p.m. No later," he instructed.

"But it's going to take us fifteen minutes to get there," Andy argued, "And the movie is an hour and a half long! What if-"

"11 pm! No later!"

"Dad!" Helen protested.

The yellow eyes shifted to her. Helen gave him her best Bambi face, but his stern look won. She sighed then grabbed onto Andy's arm.

"Okay, I'll be back by 11," she said over her shoulder, "Let's go Andy."

Mr. Medved's grip loosened, allowing Andy to slip away down the stairs. Behind him he heard something shouted in the same foreign language from before and Helen gave him a curt response. When they got in the car, he looked at the dashboard clock. 8:37 p.m.

We'll have enough time. He thought to himself.

"God, he can be such a nag!" Helen sighed as she fastened her seatbelt.

"What did he say to you back there?"

"'No hanky-panky'."

Andy sighed while his father's words repeated in the back of his head. He started the car and they were off. They zoomed half-way back towards town before making a right at a fork in the road. Helen remained quiet in the passenger seat, which did not help his anxiety.

"He sounded a little grumpier than normal," He remarked.

"Yeah, we had a fight earlier today," she explained.

"About what?"

"College."

"Ah. The midnight school or whatever?"

Just ahead was a line of cars and Andy slowed down to join them.

"Yeah, he brought it up again at breakfast," she continued, "He keeps saying the same stuff. 'They have a medical program.' 'You'll be close to home.' 'You'll fit right in.' I almost told him to fuck off but, I don't know."

The line moved forward. As they cleared the hill, he could see the giant screen of the outdoor movie theater. The only one left in the state, or so he was told. Some old-fashioned commercials for the food stand played as cars turned left into the white toll booth at the entrance.

"I mean, I know he means well but it's getting really annoying. He knows I want to go to U.M. but he keeps shoving this school in my face and I just- ARGH!"

Helen sank in her seat from the emotional overload. Andy wanted to say something but his conscious shot down every dumb question until his mind was left blank. The line moved again and they were now four cars away from the entrance. After a few moments of silence, Helen sighed.

"I'm sorry. It's just been frustrating lately," she said.

"It's fine. You needed to get it off your chest," he replied.

She turned to him with tired eyes and the corners of a smile.

"Thanks," she murmured.

Soon it was their turn to drive up. Andy pulled out his wallet and the condom slipped out. He snatched it up quickly, praying that Helen didn't notice. With a sideways glance, he saw her looking out the passenger window listlessly. He calmly pulled out the money while shoving the contraband back into his pocket before she looked back. The ticket person gave him the receipt then instructed him where to park. He drove in and went for a spot in the back corner away from everyone. There were only about two dozen cars, but they still needed to be careful.

"You hungry?" He asked.

"Not really," she replied. Andy turned his head to roll his eyes. "Could you get me a water though?"

"Yeah. I'll be right back."

He turned off the car and stepped out. The commercials kept rolling during his trek to the food stand on the other side. He could hear the sizzling of patties on the grill when he approached, and he licked his lips as he glanced at the menu. After the two people ahead of him finished their orders, it was his turn.

"Hi! What can I get for you?" The overly enthusiastic girl behind the register asked.

"I think I'll go with a hotdog, some popcorn, a coke, a water, and-," Andy looked around to make sure no one was paying attention before leaning in closer, "Are your burgers seasoned before they go on the grill?"

"Not really, no," the girl admitted sheepishly.

He nodded quickly.

"Could I get two raw patties?" He whispered.

The girl's face immediately shifted to shock then she leaned over the counter.

"What did you say?"

"Can you ring me up for two burgers but give me two raw patties?"

He could see the synapses going off in her mind before she shook her head.

"I don't think we can do that," she replied.

Andy sighed. The hangry eyes of the people behind him drilled holes in his back. He pulled out the twenty his father gave him and slipped it discreetly across the counter.

"Please?" He begged.

The girl looked down at the bill then back at him. She checked to make sure her manager was busy in the kitchen before taking it.

"Okay, I'll handle it," she whispered. Then she snapped back to her normal posture, "That's going to be fifteen dollars and eighty-six cents."

A flood of relief overcame him. He got another twenty from his wallet and handed it to her, muttering for her to keep the change, then went off to the side to wait. The movie screen suddenly paused the commercials and went black. This caught the attention of some of the people in the line but was mostly ignored. After some awkward silence, overly sinister music blared while a text crawl traveled up the screen. Andy fiddled with a straw wrapper while the scene of a woman being attacked by a tomato in her kitchen played. Right as the theme song started, he heard a hiss off to the side.

"Here you go," the register girl whispered.

A white container was slid down the counter close to his forearm. He scooped it up then turned away to check. Two pink beef patties sat inside on top of some napkins. The rest of the order soon followed. He gave the girl a smile before gathering everything up. Some of the tollbooth workers watched as he struggled the entire way back across the lot. By the time he got to his car, the movie had started proper. He sat everything on the roof while Helen looked up from her cellphone.

"That took a while," she remarked.

"I had to do some convincing," he replied.

He took the container from the top of the stack and handed it to her. Helen lifted an eyebrow as she took it. When she opened it to see what was inside, her eyes narrowed.

"You didn't have to get me anything. I said I wasn't hungry," she said.

"Mm-hm."

He handed her the water then circled around to the driver's seat. Helen sighed as she reached behind her head to undo the strings holding up her veil, letting it drop to her lap. Andy couldn't help but watch her pull back her thin lips to reveal long, pointed teeth jutting out from her gums. A serpent tongue poked out from behind them as she tore off a small piece of meat and popped it into her mouth. After that first bite, she quickly devoured both patties while Andy giggled.

"Shut up," she whined as she chewed, "So I'm a little hungrier than I thought I was."

Andy laughed then turned away to bite into his hotdog. They sat in silence, enjoying their food while the tomatoes on the screen terrorized humanity. Helen dabbed her mouth with a napkin then closed the container.

"Where should I put this?" She asked.

"Just put it on the ground, I'll clean it up later," he replied.

She shrugged and dropped the garbage by her feet. He soon finished the hotdog and placed his container with hers. With their stomachs satisfied they sat quietly as they continued to watch the film. Andy twiddled his fingers in his lap, not sure what to do with them. Beside him, he saw Helen doing the same. His ears grew warm as he prepared what to say next.

"Do you... want to move to the backseat?"

Helen's head snapped up.

"What?"

"Uh, do you want to sit in the backseat?"

"Oh. Um. Sure."

They both got out and into the backseat. At first, they stiffly stayed on their respective sides, scared out of their minds. As the movie went on, they scooted closer and closer together until they were hip to hip. Eventually, Helen rested her head on his shoulder. No matter how hard he tried, Andy could not relax. Just as he managed to push all the perverted thoughts to the back of his psyche, Helen's hand slid onto his. He turned over his hand and their fingers interlocked. Then he felt her head nuzzle into the crook of his neck as she cuddled closer. All his dirty thoughts bubbled back to the surface.

Ihaveacondomihaveacondomihaveacondomihaveacondom

"All right, you guys! They're gone now!"

The ending song blared as the credits rolled. Helen sat up to straight while they both inhaled deeply as if they'd woken up from a nap.

"What time is it?" She asked.

Andy reached into his pocket to fish out his phone. 10:42. He stared at the numbers then looked at Helen. The movie screen light glistened in her eyes and long teeth, looking like a scene from a noir film. A lie started to form on his tongue, but guilt had him turning the phone over for her to see.

"We should go," she said, "My dad will kill us if we're late."

"We could tell him there was traffic," he suggested, "He's not really going to count the seconds, is he?"

A small laugh escaped Helen's lips.

"Knowing him, he's probably sitting in the living room, staring at that old grandfather clock," she guessed, "No, we shouldn't risk it."

Andy deflated but tried not to let it show.

"Alright, let's go."

They returned to the front seats, and he started the car. Soon, they were on the road back to her house. The ride was awkward and quiet. Andy felt a growing sense of shame while Helen leaned back in her seat, twisting her veil in her lap. When he turned at the fork in the road, she finally spoke.

"I wish we could do this more often," she muttered, "It would be nice to go out to a dinner or something."

"Yeah," Andy agreed.

An image of the two of them eating pizza at the local pizzeria popped into his head; it warmed him inside. There was a short silence before she spoke again.

"I'm sorry."

"Hm? For what?"

"I don't know. It's just- I know you wanted to- never mind."

Andy felt a blush form on his face with the realization that it wasn't just him.

"No, it's not you! I'm sorry if I made you uncomfortable," he sputtered out before he could think.

"I wasn't uncomfortable," she said calmly.

"Oh."

Silence again. Andy subtly slowed the car to extend their time as much as he could.

"I wish we didn't have to be so secretive," Helen said, "If I wasn't like this, we could go to an actual movie theater. We could be in public. We could-"

She stopped then looked out the window. Andy searched his brain for something to say but, for once that night, it was blank. They turned onto the gravel driveway and up to the house. He put the car in park and just sat in his seat while Helen continued to look away. At that moment, his brain finally kicked into gear.

"Hey."

She perked up. Andy faced her, giving his best smile then held out his hand. She stared back with wide eyes before taking it.

"I never minded when I first met you and I don't mind now," he said, "I'm okay with this. Don't ever feel bad about who you are."

A weary smile broke out on her face. Then she leaned over and planted a kiss on his lips. The sudden action threw Andy's mind back into a horny frenzy. He smacked all the thoughts away just as Helen drew back to put her veil back on.

"I'll see you later," she said.

"Yeah, you too," Andy replied.

She gave him one last smile then stepped out. Andy started the car again as she walked up the steps towards the waiting open door. He squinted to see Mr. Medved for some sort of acknowledgement but the door closed the minute she was inside. He shrugged to himself then turned around to drive back home, his lips still tingling.

True Love's Release

At almost ten thirty, Phillip's cab stopped in front of the museum of natural science. He hopped out, paid the driver, and ran up the steps, hauling a brown briefcase. His thin framed glasses nearly slid off his nose with the pace he was going. Finally, he reached the security guard at the door and pulled out his work ID to show him.

"You're pretty late today, Phillip," the guard remarked, "Late night, late start?"

"Oh yeah," Phillip replied with a yawn.

"Better hurry up or Talia will get worried."

Phillip ignored the comment and rushed inside. The ticket collector waved to him as he passed, and he nodded back. He weaved through the crowd of visitors towards the corridor lined with posters reading "Sleeping Beauty". Just as he was about to enter the backrooms, he heard someone call his name. Glancing to his left, he spotted Charlette waving to him while a group of school children followed her.

No no no no no, he thought as she led the small army up to him.

"Everyone, this is Dr. Phillip Coser," Charlette explained loudly, "He's the head scientist investigating the mystery of our 'Sleeping Beauty'."

All the students looked up at him in awe, making him slightly uncomfortable.

"Can you stick around for a bit?" She asked him with a pleading look in her eye.

Again, he mentally screamed 'no' but the flurry of questions began before he could answer.

"Is she really Sleeping Beauty?" One little boy spouted.

"Well, we don't know for sure but there is some speculation that she may have been the inspiration for the legend," Phillip answered through a fake smile.

"How's she still alive? Shouldn't she be dead?" A girl asked.

"We're trying to figure that out too. Right now, we're running some tests to find how she has managed to stay asleep for so long-"

"You mean she's never woken up?" A voice from the back shouted.

"No, she has not woken up since she was discovered-"

"Even when you kissed her?" The little girl asked.

He stopped then looked at the curious face with a blank mind.

"Huh?"

"In the story, the only thing that can wake her up is true love's kiss. It's the only thing that can break the evil witch's spell."

Phillip looked over to the equally flustered Charlotte then back to the girl, taking in a deep breath.

"Well, we can't do that. We're interested in the scientific reasoning for why she's remained asleep," he explained as best as he could.

"Plus!" Charlotte butted in, "Dr. Coser isn't a prince. Only a prince could wake her up in the story."

"Oh yeah," the girl said.

"Okay, thank you for talking with us Dr. Coser. Let's move on now!"

She herded the children away while Phillip disappeared through the double doors. As he made his way through the maze of hallways, he felt a hand smack his back.

"Dr. Coser is late to work today? Is the world coming to an end?"

"Hey Max," Phillip replied.

His friend gave him a huge mocking grin.

"What happened? Traffic?"

"No, I stayed up all night going over the reports and slept through my alarm."

"If you had a smartphone, you could've set multiple alarms," Max pointed out, "Maybe it's time to trade in that dinosaur brick of yours for something from the twenty-first century?"

"Some of us prefer not to have an NSA spy in our pocket."

"Hey, at least we're never alone! By the way, Dr. Basile will be here at around eleven for his visit."

"That's today? I thought he wasn't coming until next month."

"We were only given a year to examine her. They're starting to get antsy about us having her for so long."

Phillip bit his inner cheek then sighed.

"Okay. I'm going to go check on her before he comes."

"Don't get too handsy!"

"Shut up!"

Max laughed and jogged back over to the geology department. Phillip picked up his pace over to the "special feature" wing, making his way down to the last door on the left. Medical machines lined the walls of the room, each one making their own noises. In the middle of the beeping and blinking equipment was a hospital bed where a girl lay motionless. Her hair was a beautiful golden color, her skin was creamy white, and her lips were so perfectly pink that they looked painted on. She slept soundly while attached to various machines, undisturbed by the world.

Phillip stared at her for a few moments then set his briefcase down on the nearby counter. After hanging his jacket on the door hook, he opened the briefcase to pull out the various reports he had typed out the night before. Once he was somewhat organized, he pulled out his iPod to select an album and hooked it up to the nearby speaker. The sounds of fifes and lutes soon filled the room as he picked up a clipboard and went over to the girl's side.

"Hello Talia," he whispered with a small smile, "I'm sorry I'm late."

He then went through the routine of checking all the machines, changing out the IV bag attached to her arm, and looking for any physical changes. When all of that was out of the way, he set the clipboard aside and reached over to fluff her pillow. A few strands of her hair fell to graze the back of his hand, making his heart to skip a beat. Suddenly, the door opened and the museum director Ms. Rogers stepped in with an old man following her. Phillip stopped what he was doing to face them.

"Good morning Dr. Coser," she greeted, "I heard you were running behind this morning."

"Um, yes. Had some trouble with my alarm this morning," Phillip mumbled, "I finished the report on the blood and bone analysis last night."

"Excellent, I would like to see that on my desk before lunch," she cheerfully replied, "Let me introduce you to Dr. Basile from the Italian archeology association. Dr. Basile, this is Dr. Coser. He's been in charge of the research done on Talia."

Dr. Basile smiled and reached out to shake.

"It's a pleasure to meet you sir!" Phillip said, "I've read your book on Talia and other artifacts you found in her castle. It was very useful for my own research."

"I'm glad to hear that. That book is my pride and joy," Dr. Basile replied, "And I see you have taken good care of our beauty."

All Phillip could manage was a meek nod. Footsteps rushed towards the door, and they were met with three female staff members.

"Please excuse us but we need to get her ready for the exhibit," one of them explained.

"Come in, we were just about to leave anyways," Ms. Rogers said.

The women entered with their makeup cart. Phillip gathered his report from the counter and turned off the music before following the other two.

"What was that you were playing in there?" Dr. Basile inquired.

"I collected a couple albums of medieval music to play while we conducted our studies," Phillip explained, "I figured that, if she were listening, it would make her feel more at home while she was with us."

"How thoughtful," Dr. Basile remarked, "It seems we have chosen the right man for the job."

"We have ensured the absolute comfort and security for Talia," Ms. Rogers butted in.

Phillip felt a pinch of anger but kept his mouth shut as they continued down the hall. A temp worker came from the other direction and Ms. Rogers stopped him.

"Could you please give Dr. Basile a tour of our laboratories while I talk with Dr. Coser for a minute?" She asked sweetly.

"Yes ma'am. Follow me sir."

They strolled down the hall, the temp stiff with nerves. As soon as they rounded the corner, Ms. Rogers turned to Phillip, her cheesy smile vanished.

"Coser, do we have any new data on Talia to keep her here a while longer?"

After taking a deep breath, Phillip shook his head.

"Blood and bone tests indicate that she was born around 1100 AD and her brain scans came back normal. Even the examination of her organs came back normal, just like the other reports," he explained, "We still have no idea how she's avoided aging or how she's still alive. We're no closer to cracking this mystery than they were twenty years ago."

"Damn!" Ms. Rogers hissed, "We're going to lose our most popular exhibit! Do you understand that?"

Again, Phillip felt his anger rise but before he could defend himself, she turned away.

"We'll just have to hope that Dr. Basile will put in a good word with the Italian government so she can stay," she sighed, "I'm going to lunch. See if you can find any new information at all."

With that, she stormed off, leaving Phillip alone with clenched fists.

"She's not just an exhibit," he fumed quietly as he left.

He slipped out into the public area, head buzzing and stomach growling. Just as he was about to leave the building, he looked over to the crowd of children and adults gathered around a giant window. Charlette was desperately trying to spout facts over the excited crowd as the curtain rose to reveal the main attraction. Phillip walked over, maneuvering around people to get a glimpse. There was Talia, all made up and wearing a flowing purple princess dress, lying on a plush bed in front of a painted background of a castle. Her calm face soothed whatever fire burned in his stomach. Even in the chaotic crowd, he felt as if he were melting in her presence.

Some of the patrons bumped him, shaking him back to reality. He straightened his spotted tie, smoothed over his brown hair, then turned to leave for lunch. Before he left the room, he saw Dr. Basile with the temp. The poor boy was trying to prattle on with information about the museum while the doctor stared at Talia. A creeping feeling went up Phillip's spine, but he pushed it out of his head.

Within a half-hour, he had a sub sandwich and was plopped in front of a computer in the back. Between bites, he combed over the data, the charts, texts, and even photos of samples taken. He opened every file on Talia or anything related to her, even after his sandwich was long gone. After some time, his fingers grew numb. He tried to keep going but his eyes started drooping, forcing him to take a coffee break. As he used the restroom and got himself a cup of barely tolerable coffee from the breakroom, he thought of other ways to spin the results to sound more impressive. But when he returned to the computer, his mind was empty and he felt nothing but dread. Still, he kept searching for something, for any possible breakthrough. He was just getting back into the zone when he felt fingers tickle his sides. He jolted upright, nearly falling out of his chair as he heard Charlotte laugh hysterically from behind him.

"Jesus! Don't scare me like that!" He scolded.

"I'm sorry, I couldn't help it," she giggled, "Max told me you were in here so I came to say goodnight before I left."

"Huh? Night?"

He looked at the time at the bottom of his computer screen. It was 9:48 pm.

"That explains why I'm nodding off," he groaned, removing his glasses to rub his eyes, "I still have to do my nightly checks on Talia before I go."

He started saving documents and closing out of the computer when he noticed that Charlotte was still staring at him.

"Is there something else you wanted?" He asked.

"I'm just wondering what you're gonna do when she's gone," she replied.

"What do you mean?"

"Ever since she got here, she's been the center of your world. What will you do when she goes back to Italy?"

"You make it sound like I'm infatuated with her."

"You are, though! For the past year all you've done was study her and take care of her. You go out of your way for her to the point of obsession. You won't even take on an assistant to help you. It's like you want her all to yourself or something."

Phillip hid his embarrassed face as he pulled his flash drive out from the computer.

"I-It's my job to look after her. She's a valuable part of the museum," he explained, "It was inevitable that she would go back to her home country eventually. But I would be lying if I said that I wouldn't miss her...."

The words were bitter on his tongue. He shook away the feeling as he packed up his things. Charlotte waited for him to say more then sighed.

"I give up. You're hopeless," she muttered, "Goodnight Phillip."

"Huh? What does that mean?"

She just smiled sadly before leaving the room. Phillip thought about what she said for a moment but disregarded it as he stood up to leave, tossing his trash in the bin before walking out. As he went through the empty hallways, he spotted Max standing by the coffee machine in the breakroom.

"You too?" He asked as he passed.

"These new analysis machines are a pain in the ass!" Max groaned, "We haven't even gotten half the samples done yet."

Phillip gave him a nod in solidarity then continued on his way to Talia's room. Before he stepped through the doorframe, he stopped. There Dr. Basile stood by Talia's side, holding her hand and singing a quiet song to her. He stared in disbelief as his briefcase slipped out of his fingers and crashed to the ground. Dr. Basile quickly dropped her hand and turned to him.

"Oh, forgive me. I didn't hear you," he said.

"N-no, it's okay," Phillip replied, "I just came by to do my last check on her for the night."

Dr. Basile nodded and stepped aside. Philip picked up his briefcase to set on the counter before getting his clipboard. He made his usual rounds checking the machines while keeping an eye on the other man in the room. He stooped down to take a sample of her blood when Dr. Basile finally spoke.

"You know, twenty years ago I would never have considered that the fairy tales we tell our children could be real," he said with a chuckle, "When I was called to the site, I had already made up my mind that magic didn't exist."

Phillip looked up to see him smiling at the ground.

"I still remember the first time I saw her castle, all covered in vines and thorns. When she was discovered, we thought she was one of the villagers who snuck inside somehow. It wasn't until we couldn't wake her that we realized who she was."

The two of them stood in awkward silence. Phillip looked at Talia's face, imagining her in the abandoned castle with the rotten dress he had seen in old photographs. After a couple of minutes, he cleared his throat.

"In the story, it says that an evil fairy's spell kept her from aging," he explained, "If I was a believer, I would say that it also kept her alive all these years. But I'm a scientist so that theory's out of the question."

"She does make you wonder, doesn't she?" Dr. Basile chuckled, "But I pity her."

"Hm?"

"For over nine hundred years she's been in a deep slumber. Everyone she's ever known is dead; she didn't even have the chance to know what true love felt like. Now she is only an artifact to be admired and studied."

".... I wish I knew how to wake her."

The old man looked over to him and smiled.

"You love her, don't you?" He asked.

"Wh- No! That's not what I meant!" Phillip gawked, "It's just that- If she were awake, she could have her own life and not be treated like an object."

Dr. Basile laughed and Phillip looked away, red in the face.

"There's no need to be bashful," he said, "I was in the same predicament myself when I saw her. She's the only one who had me questioning my love for my wife."

Phillip quickly took the sample of blood, jotted down the rest of the information needed on the clipboard and placed it on the counter.

"Er- If you'll excuse me, I need to examine the body for any abnormal changes," he muttered.

There were a few seconds of silence before Dr. Basile nodded and turned to leave.

"You've taken such good care of her, Dr. Coser. I wish you could come back with us to continue the research," he said, "It's a shame we couldn't wake her. I'm sure she would have loved to meet you."

With that, he walked out of the room. Phillip waited for the sound of his footsteps to disappear before doing the full body examination. No new changes, which he noted on her chart. As he redressed her, he glanced over at her face. His eyes traced her perfectly beautiful features, lingering on her lips. There was a small smudge of lipstick left from when her makeup was removed. He used his thumb to wipe it off the best he could. Before he could process what he was about to do, he leaned down and kissed her gently. His hand reached up to hold the side of her face as he kissed her more deeply. A ticklish sensation went through his body as he slipped into a state of absolute bliss. Then, as if he were hit by lightning, he jumped back, realizing what he had done.

"God damn it!" He shuttered, "I'm horrible."

He looked up at the clock on the other side of the wall which now read 10:27.

I need to leave before I do something dumber, he thought.

At that moment, he heard a gasp as if someone had just come up for air. He looked down at Talia, but she looked no different from a second ago.

"Great, now I'm hallucinating," he grunted.

He put the blood sample in the mini fridge under the counter then picked up his briefcase. Before he left, he made sure to tuck Talia snuggly into bed. The urge to kiss her again arose but he batted the idea away and walked towards the door, turning off the lights as he went.

"Goodnight Talia," he whispered.

He slunk down the hall and through the museum to get outside, overwhelmed with embarrassment and shame. The streets were pretty much empty, but he still managed to flag down a cab. Once he got in and gave his address, he slouched into the seat and stared out the window. He was about to zone out when his phone rang; the ringtone indicating it was Max. He sighed and opened his flip phone.

"Yeah?" He answered.

"Dude, you have to come back here!" Max shouted, "Something happened to Talia!"

"What? What happened?" Phillip gasped, sitting up in his seat.

"I don't know! I heard someone scream from your department and when I got there I saw Dr. Basile having a panic attack-"

"Call the director right now! I'll be right over!" Phillip ordered before hanging up and turning to the driver. "I need you to turn around!"

"Calm down man, I got it," the cabby muttered.

The car screeched as it did a one-eighty back to the museum. Once it stopped, Phillip threw him twenty and jumped out. He ran back up the steps, nearly tripping several times, and burst into the building. Dr. Basile was sitting on a bench by the entrance, trembling with a cup of water in his hand. A security guard stood next to him, comforting him. Phillip left them be and ran to the backrooms where he found Max white as a sheet.

"What's going on?" Phillip demanded.

"I don't know. I mean- I- come here," he stammered.

The two of them scurried down the hall, with Phillip pulling ahead. When he turned into Talia's room, he screamed. There lay a grey, decomposing skeleton in the hospital bed where Talia once was. Its bones were cracked and crumbling with dried out hair circling the skull.

"What the hell is this?!" Phillip screamed, "What kind of sick joke is this?"

Max looked at him in silence, not knowing what to say. Phillip rushed over to the bed to examine the corpse. The monitors that were attached to it were all blank. As the gravity of the situation settled in, he barely noticed the tears that streamed down his cheeks.

"Oh god," he croaked, "Talia......"

Loud clacking heels came storming down the hallway and Ms. Rogers burst into the room, red in the face.

"What the hell is going on?" She yelled.

Phillip simply turned to face her then stepped out of the way. Her eyes widened as soon as she saw the skeleton.

"This had better be a prank," she said.

He shook his head slowly.

"What happened? What did you do to her?" She demanded.

"I- I don't know," Phillip stammered, "All I did was take a blood sample and-"

A lightbulb went off in his head. He rushed over to the mini fridge to retrieve the sample, but it had turned black and crusty. He looked back to Ms. Rogers who was leaning on the counter for support.

"We're in deep shit," she muttered, "Call the police and get everyone in the department here now. I'll call the other board members."

Phillip and Max nodded and scrambled to do as they were told. Within half an hour, five policemen were there along with several lab techs to analyze the remains. The police began their investigation while Ms. Rogers and the board tried to figure out what to do next. To Phillip, it was all white noise; he felt too sick to help the others. Instead, he wandered aimlessly through the hallways, thoughts plagued with Talia. Eventually, he found himself back at the Sleeping Beauty exhibit. The posters of her lovely face broke his heart even more.

"Oh god, why?" He cried.

"I don't think God had anything to do with this."

Dr. Basile walked up next to him as Phillip looked down in defeat.

"I'm so sorry," he muttered.

"For what?" Dr. Basile asked.

"I- I've let you down. I let Talia down. I was in charge of keeping her safe and this happened to her. Please forgive me."

Dr. Basile only stared ahead.

"You never told me if you found anything," he stated coldly.

Phillip turned to him in shock.

"Y-you want to hear this now?" he balked.

The old Italian man nodded solemnly. Phillip shifted in his spot uncomfortably then cleared his throat.

"We couldn't find anything new," he admitted, "All the tests we ran on her gave us the same exact results as you guys and we never found the reason for her coma or her survival. But that doesn't matter now."

"I see," Dr. Basile replied, "I was afraid of that. But I'm glad."

"Glad?"

Like a ghost, Dr. Basile walked over to the poster of Talia laying on her display bed. Phillip followed him hesitantly.

"When I realized who she was, I was thrilled and excited to try to unlock the secrets behind her slumber. But as the years went by, I realized that she was no longer considered a person. To the world she was only a thing to be studied," he explained, "I secretly prayed that one day she will pass on. A pure and innocent beauty like her didn't deserve to be kept in laboratories under observation. At least now, she's free."

His words echoed in Phillip's ears.

"Yeah," he said, "I guess that makes sense."

"May I ask you something else, Dr. Coser?"

"Yes."

"Ms. Rogers informed me that you took a sample of her blood before you left. Was that the only thing you did to her aside from the physical inspection?"

Immediately, Phillip's blood turned cold.

"Y-Yes," he said quickly.

The minute the word left his lips, he felt disgusted. Dr. Basile looked him in the eye then sighed.

"I already contacted my superiors back home. They'll be here to collect the remains as soon as they can," he said, turning to walk away.

"What are you going to do with her?" Phillip asked.

"They're no longer interested in her now that she's reverted back to her natural state," Dr. Basile explained, "I plan on laying her to rest near the castle where she was found. Since I was head of the archeological study, I feel it is my duty to give her that at least."

"I-is it possible for me to attend her funeral?"

"If you want to come, you may. However, from what I can tell, you're going to be very busy for a while."

Phillip averted his eyes. Dr. Basile walked towards the exit of the museum then stopped.

"I'm sure she would have wanted to see your face before she passed," he said over his shoulders, "Farewell, Dr. Coser."

Then he left without looking back. Phillip continued to stare at Talia's picture on the wall, the lump in his throat growing bigger. Unable to take it anymore, he fell to his knees and started to sob.

A Winter Scene

White little specks drifted downward from the navy-blue void of the night, swirling in the gentle wind and dancing under the orange streetlamps. He watched them from his bedroom window, keeping his breath faint so as not to fog up the glass. His eyes tried to follow each little snowflake as they glided through the air. Beautifully, gracefully. They twirled like tiny ballerinas putting on a performance. Sparkling little dancers, just for him. He'd watch them forever if he could.

A series of fleshy thuds made their way up the stairs. He almost didn't hear them in his enchantment. Almost. The thuds made their way to the tiny door for his tiny room at the end of the hall. Without warning or hesitation, the flimsy wood burst open, banging on the wall like so many times before. There stood his mother, her spherical form stuffed into a Margaritaville hoodie and jeans. Her face was caked in gaudy makeup that tried to replicate the county-fair queen she used to be many years ago. When she spotted him, she sneered.

"Hiding again, you lazy turd? Hurry up and get the car started!"

The man paused, his mind lagging to understand the sudden order.

"What the hell are you waiting for? Get out there!"

At the last shriek, he was on his feet, legs still aching from the day's shift. He removed the blue vest he forgot he was still wearing and tossed it on the cot he called a bed. As he exited his own room, he could feel the familiar glare of contempt his mother was shooting him. He was numb to it by this point, ignoring it as he passed the old picture on the wall of her with a man he had never met but unfortunately looked like. He descended the stairs like an obedient dog to the living room where his two teenaged sisters lounged, putting on their faces like washed up clowns, in their ripped jeans from Goodwill. They threw him an insult as he passed by and giggled to themselves. He didn't bother saying anything as he grabbed his coat before exiting the barely warm home.

The freezing air stung his cheeks. It was winter, after all, just nature doing her thing. He trudged through the foot of snow to the beat up mini-van parked on the street. Before he unlocked the driver's door, he looked up. The snow still fell like feathers. Their crystal bodies shone in the light so flawlessly. He smiled as some brushed his face, giving him soft cold kisses. Affection from his little dancers. If only he could stay for a while longer. His conscious snapped back to reality, and he got into the van; starting up the ancient engine to let it warm up. Ten minutes passed as he watched his dancers through the cracked windshield. Then the sisters came out to pile into the back seats, followed but their mother waddling to the passenger side. He put the van in drive, and they were off.

All the bickering and squabbling and jeers were tuned out as he drove away from the isolated neighborhood onto the country road. It was all white noise to him. Instead, he focused on the unplowed road, carefully maneuvering through the fresh fluff. The steep hill came, and he sat up alert with his foot steady as they climbed. At one point his eyes veered to the left to see the dead cornfield, now a vast plain of frozen cotton. A white blanket that stretched out for miles. He wished he could lie in it and forget the world.

"Watch the road you idiot!" His mother hissed.

His gaze snapped back to the road in front of him. They were at the sharp turn at the very top of the hill. He twisted the steering wheel to the right just in time and they made it. There were cackles from the back and a huff from the passenger side. They continued on their way, winding down the snow-covered road to their destination: the old diner at the edge of town. He parked as close to the entrance as he could for a Friday night. There were still grumbles of disappointment as the women got out and scurried out of the cold.

Somehow, they were seated in the packed house and their drink orders were taken. The waitress smiled through the rude comments until she got to him. She was a familiar face, maybe from high school, with a petite frame and strawberry blonde hair. He hated that he couldn't remember her, despite seeing her nametag. He ordered his Coke then went back to staring at the menu that he practically memorized. Everything around him blurred together in a fog of noise. Knives scrapping plates, glasses clunking together, incomprehensible conversations from the other tables. Each sound irritated him. He wanted to go back outside, back to the quiet and snow. But, at least, the women around him were leaving him alone; prattling to each other about local gossip.

The drinks were set down on the table, making him jump a little. His sisters immediately start off with their orders as the waitress scrambled to write everything down on her pad. He kept his head down, knowing better than to try to compete for attention. When the waitress came to him, he cleared his throat to speak.

"The chicken strips?" She guessed before he could say anything.

He looked up to her in amazement; that was exactly what he wanted. She giggled and gave him a smile, a genuine smile. Everything went quiet to him as if they were suddenly thrown into a pocket dimension. Suddenly, a few memories resurfaced of the girl in art club with the big, fluffy sweaters. She was always the odd one out but that's what made her so intriguing. He smiled back and opened his mouth.

"That's enough," his mother grunted.

The diner sounds came back in full force. He and she were no longer alone. She glanced behind him and got a look of fear, he already knew what she saw. He confirmed the order so she could escape to the kitchen. Some teasing comments were made at his expense as he felt the stabbing glare of his mother on him. A short time later, the food was out. The waitress didn't stay long, and he didn't blame her. They ate while the sisters gushed about the men they spotted all around them. His mother didn't mind this, she never did. He nibbled on his chicken strips in silence, not bothering to ask for sauce. The check came. Mother begrudgingly paid without tipping. They finished quickly then rushed out without a word.

Rose gold hair was still on his mind as he started up the van again. He looked through the front window to catch a glimpse of her, but she was lost in the crowd. His body moved automatically to put the van in reverse and get out of the parking lot. To his right, his mother went on and on about her humiliation back there. He should have known better than to flirt with the wait-staff and make a scene and he only wanted a pretty face. Etc. The backseat audience listened on with amusement as they stared at their phones. He took it, just like always.

The snow fell harder now. It speckled the pitch-black darkness in front of him. Their plump bodies weren't graceful anymore; now they were plummeting down like agents on a rescue mission. He squinted as he looked ahead, trying to hold back a tear, as the van approached the turn at the top of the hill. Then, he felt something click. It came from somewhere deep in his skull, close to the back of his brain. Everything felt warm all of the sudden as his eyes relaxed and his foot pressed harder on the gas. The old van accelerated as best as it could while trying not to lose traction. The turn got closer and closer at an exponential rate.

"Slow down, you idiot! You'll get us all killed!" His mother barked without looking up from her phone.

Her voice simply echoed in his ears as if she were talking at the other end of a tunnel. His foot kept pressing, nothing was stopping it now. The van roared as it kept up with the increasing speed.

"I said slow down!"

"Yeah moron! Are you trying to hurry so you can go beat off or something?"

Some awkward laughter came from the back. He didn't care; his foot was on the floor now. The headlights were looking past the edge of the hill, running out into the dark oblivion of night.

"Hit the brakes!" His mother shrieked.

Too late. The front bumper burst through the rusty guardrail with little resistance. His mother looked over to him in a panic, silently pleading for answers. But all she could see in his tired eyes was pure, fiery hatred; the last thing she would ever see. The weight in the front forced the van into an instant nosedive. Three screams of horror erupted in the van. The first crash banged his face onto the steering wheel, but he felt no pain. Nor did he feel the other crashes and they tumbled down to the white field below. By the time his mind came back into focus, it was over.

It was quiet now. He thought there would be more noise but there wasn't. There was only the winter wind whistling outside. He turned to the right to look at his mother. Her face was smashed into the dashboard, not moving at all, with blood splattered everywhere. A fuzzy feeling of relief started to buzz throughout his body. He climbed out of the shattered window, only now noticing that the van was upside down. When he got out, he studied the crumpled-up metal in front of him. It looked like a balled-up Christmas chocolate wrapper. He looked up at the hill with the busted railing. It didn't seem so big now.

The cold wind brushed his cheek, beckoning him to look in the other direction. There wasn't any light anymore, allowing the black sky to return to the peaceful navy ocean of eternity. The snow waltzed around him, kissing his rosy cheeks before melting in with his tears of joy. He was finally home. The wind whipped again, begging him to follow. A smile stretched across his face as he took the first step. He walked through the field with his beautiful white dancers, leaving the cries of agony behind him.

The Boatman

Pulling out the drawers of the cheap wooden dresser, Chester tossed out the clothing in search of any valuables to take. He eventually found a few necklaces and coins under the garments and threw them into his carpet bag. Satisfied with his haul, Chester closed his bag and looked back at the woman on the bed. She was naked with her wrists and ankles bound together in twine, bruised and crying. Chester smiled cruelly to her and tipped his hat.

"Thanks for the fun, sweetheart," he sneered, "Next time, don't let in a stranger."

He smacked her bottom before walking out of the room, stepping on her torn dress as he went. The rest of the house was also a mess from his looting, but he didn't care as he grabbed a coat from the closet before leaving. The humid twilight air hit him as soon as he stepped out. A couple passing by looked at him curiously. Chester simply tipped his hat then strolled down the dirt road. Nobody else paid much attention to him, allowing him to relax. After a few minutes of walking, he made it to the docks on the river. He scanned the area and spotted a cargo ferry loading up. Straightening his tie, he approached one of the workers and waiting for him to notice him.

"Excuse me, sir. Where is this ferry headed?" He asked.

"New Orleans," the worker grunted.

"That's where I need to be. Would you mind if I hopped aboard? I'll pay you for your troubles," Chester offered.

"We're not a passenger boat," the worker replied.

"Oh, come now. One person won't be too much trouble."

"The answer is no. Beat it!"

Chester was about to say something else, but the worker scowled at him, showing no signs of letting up. Back on the main street, he heard someone call for the police. Panicked, he looked up stream and saw a narrow boat approaching. The single man who was pushing the boat along with a pole was draped in tattered rags and a wide brimmed hat that hid most of his face. Chester waved to him out of desperation.

"Hello! Could you possibly take me to New Orleans?" He shouted.

The driver didn't say anything, almost like he was ignoring him, but slowly steered his boat towards the docks and stopped right in front of him.

"Thank you, sir," Chester gasped as he climbed aboard, "I was getting sick of this hick town. How much do you charge?"

"I do not require payment," the boatman replied in a monotone voice.

"Suit yourself then."

They were about to move away when loud thumping steps pounded on the dock towards them.

"Hold it right there!" A voice shouted.

The boatman froze in place. Chester gritted his teeth and reached for the revolver he kept on his waist. He soon relaxed when he saw it was an overweight old man and a thinner, younger man carrying a large suitcase. He slumped in his seat as the pair hurried over.

"Excuse me, but could you take one more passenger?" the fat man gasped, "The driver who was supposed to take my son to university never showed and he needs to be there by tomorrow."

"I already have a passenger," the boatman replied.

"Please, have a heart," the fat man begged, "I'll pay handsomely."

As he argued with the boatman, Chester noticed that more police were running through the streets.

"Is the university close to New Orleans?" He quickly asked the thin boy.

"I-it's just a little south from here, i-in the same direction," the boy answered.

"I don't mind sharing the ride," Chester said, looking over to the driver.

The boatman was silent for a second then nodded his head. The fat man sighed in relief and quickly gave the town name as the boy climbed in.

"Thank you so much," the fat man said, "how much do I owe you?"

"I do not require payment," the boatman replied.

"Really? Are you sure? Alright then. Good luck, my boy! Make me proud!"

"I w-will father," the boy replied.

With the boy settled in, suitcase between his legs, the boatman pushed away from the dock and headed down stream. Chester breathed a sigh of relief when the town was out of sight and looked around casually. The boy sat nervously, twiddling his thumbs. This annoyed Chester but he brushed it off as he got comfortable in his seat.

"L-lovely night," the boy spouted out of nowhere.

"M-hmm," Chester hummed.

"So, are y-you a salesman or s-something?"

"Of sorts."

"W-what do you s-sell?"

Chester groaned internally but decided to entertain the boy so as not to look suspicious.

"Jewelry," he replied. He reached into his carpetbag and pulled out one of the stolen necklaces. "See?"

"O-oh, that's n-neat," the boy said, "B-but aren't you sc-scared of being robbed?"

"I'm not too worried," Chester answered with a smirk, "What are you going to university for?"

"I-I'm going for l-l-law."

"A lawyer?"

"Y-yes."

"You'll need to fix that stutter, or you'll annoy every judge in the country."

"I-I know."

The boy looked down at the water in shame. Their boat drifted down the river in silence except for the chirping of insects and splashing water around them. Chester eyed the boy's suitcase, wondering what was inside. His hand quietly went back up to his revolver.

No one's around to see. I'll just need to take care of the driver. He thought.

"We're here," the boatman announced.

Both Chester and the boy looked up confused. To their right was a dock much bigger than the one they had left, with numerous people running around.

"T-this can't be right," the boy gawked, "W-we shouldn't be there until morning."

"This is the place you requested to be taken," the boatman said flatly.

Chester looked at some of the signs around the port and saw that they were, in fact, in a different town. The boatman steered to an open space where the boy stepped out.

"I-I don't know how you d-did that but t-thank you," he said, turning to leave.

"Wait," the boatman commanded.

He pulled his ragged cloak aside to reveal a wooden chest, which neither of them had noticed, bolted to the boat between his feet. The boatman opened it to reveal that it was filled to the brim with gold coins and jewels. Chester stared in shock as the boatman picked out a few gold coins and handed them to the boy, shutting the chest with his bare foot.

"Take these," he said.

"O-oh n-no, you r-really do have to give me those," the boy gasped, "I-if anything, I should be paying y-you."

"Take it," the boatman insisted, "This gold should only go to those who deserve it."

The boy looked uneasy but took the coins anyways.

"T-thank you," he muttered.

The boatman gave him a nod then pushed away from the dock. Chester watched the boy stare after them before walking towards the town. A few minutes later, they were back in the dense forest trees, traveling in silence. Chester looked back at the boatman in astonishment. It took him some time before he could say anything.

"You don't seem like that type of man to have any valuables on you," he started, "Why are you giving them away? You could quit this business and live in luxury."

"This is my punishment for the crimes I have committed," the boatman answered.

"What crimes?"

"There are...too many to recount."

Chester continued to size him up. Never had he met someone who'd offer up such information willingly. An idea came to mind, and he gripped his revolver again.

"Listen, friend, how about we make a deal? You give me the chest and I won't alert the police. What do you say?"

"This gold cannot go to a man as cruel as you."

"Wha-What did you say?" Chester demanded.

"I know of the deeds you've done. An hour ago, you raped and robbed a woman like you have done many times before."

Chester felt his body grow cold.

"How do you know that?" He hissed, "Are you a cop or something?"

"I am not an officer."

"Then how the hell do you know about me?"

"I know the deeds of all who step onto this boat. From beggars to merchants, I see it all."

Without another thought, Chester pulled out his revolver and pointed it at the boatman shooting him twice square on. However, the boatman continued to push forward as if nothing happened. It was then that Chester noticed that the world around him was going by faster and the boat began to wobble from the increased speed.

"I see the souls of all those who ride this boat. The pure ones I take to their destinations safely. The cruel ones I take to him."

Everything around them became a blur while the wind picked up. Chester dropped his revolver to hold onto the sides of the boat. A red glow started to shine in front of them with shadows dancing in it.

"Let me out of this thing!" He screamed.

The boatman kept staring ahead, driving them towards the light.

"I cannot rest until all the gold is gone, until all souls go where they need to be."

From the red glow came the gapping mouth of a large beast. Fire jumped out from between its teeth while demons danced on its tongue. At the back of its throat there were screams of pain and agony. Before Chester could jump out, the boatman grabbed him by the collar and held him up in the air.

"This is where you belong," the boatman cried.

He then tossed him like a ragdoll directly into the beast's mouth. Chester screamed as the fire burned away his clothes and the demons pulled him towards the back of the throat. When he was far enough in, the beast's mouth closed and disappeared back into the water. The boat slowed to a normal pace and the sound of insects returned to the boatman's ears. He reached down to pick up the revolver left behind. After examining it, he tossed it into the water along with the carpet bag. Both sunk quickly as he pushed on. Soon, he was in New Orleans; illuminated by lamplights and still as busy as ever. On one of the docks, a woman in a long pink dress waved to him. He steered towards her and stopped.

"Thank goodness I spotted you! I thought I would never find someone this late to take me upriver," she said as she climbed aboard with a burlap sack in hand, "How much do you charge?"

"I do not require payment," the boatman replied.

She gave him a puzzled look but shrugged and told him her destination. He nodded and pushed away from the dock, heading back up the river.

A Night on the Town

Ding

The small chime broke Tammy out of her buzzed daydream. She rummaged through her purse to grab her cellphone and tapped the screen. It was a new text message.

[Robyn: Sorry for the late reply! I just got an email saying that I'm supposed to do a presentation tomorrow. :(I hope you have a good night out though!]

Tammy stared at the words for a moment before her fingers glided over the keyboard to type a response.

[It's okay. My boss sprung something on me at the last minute too. Argh! We'll just have to catch up over drinks later :)]

[Robyn: If we get the time lol. I'm not sure when I'll be free, but I'll keep you posted. Happy birthday by the way!]

[Lol Thank you!]

She was about to put in a heart emoji like she normally would but wasn't in the mood for it. After she hit send, she held onto the phone for another minute before slipping it back into her purse. She reached for the pint in front of her to take another sip. It was her fourth one that evening. Some of the bar workers were giving her a side eye but quickly ignored her to tend to the unusually large Tuesday night crowd. The all-girl party at the end of the bar finally started to calm down while some businessmen chatted among themselves. Tammy thought she recognized one of them but couldn't place his face.

Her gaze dropped down to the file she managed to complete an hour ago just after her second beer. She almost managed to escape the office after a grueling day of staring at her computer screen and filling out forms. Almost. But Sean just had to stop her before she cleared the cubicles; trying to chat her up like every other day. The manager happened to notice that she was so free and ahead of everything so it only made sense to give her the giant folder that needed to be completed by tomorrow. It was the most obvious conclusion. The cherry on top was the box of chocolates from the man who caused this.

"A special gift for your special day."

Remembering that phrase coming from his tuna smelling mouth made Tammy shiver in disgust. The box sat next to the file, unopened. A worn-out thought to report him to HR popped up again but she bottled it away; it wasn't worth the headache. Instead, she took another gulp of her beer to wash the idea away before she dwelled on it further.

To distract herself, she pulled out her phone again to check for updates. A few Facebook messages wishing her a 'happy birthday' popped up. She tapped on the app to scroll through the generic well-wishes with maybe a few XOs thrown in to show extra love. Her parents sent their regards from their Florida vacation. Grandma sent her love from the hospital she was checked in; her third stay that year. Tammy swallowed the last of her beer and exited the app to go back to her messages.

[April: I'm sorry I can't tonight! Life's been super crazy lately!]

[It's fine. We can try another time]

[Diana: I'm sorry but Lily got sick and something just came up. Happy birthday though!]

[Thank you! Maybe we can get together this weekend?]

[Todd: I hate to do this but I'm going to have to stay in tonight. Work has worn me out and my back is acting up. Hope you have a good night]

[I'll try. :) Take care of yourself so we can try again another time]

That was it, everyone was busy. Todd's message reminded her of the pain in her lower back and feet from the weeks of overtime. Despite this, her skirt felt tighter and even her blouse and hosiery were more constricting than usual. She looked up at the bar clock. Just a little past midnight, way later than she intended on staying out. She flagged down one of the bartenders for her check. With bill paid, coat on, and file gathered, she was out the door.

The cold January air didn't bother her at first; the alcohol kept her belly and nose feeling cozy. But soon the icy temperature penetrated her coat, working its way to her bones. Tammy hugged herself as she briskly made her way down the ten-block journey to her apartment. Then she would go to sleep, wake up in a few hours, go to work and continue the whole cycle all over again. For the rest of her life.

She stopped halfway through the crosswalk on a strangely barren street. Filing out papers, extra work, creepy coworkers, just to keep on with life as is. Forever. She shook the thought from her head to clear the rest of the distance as fast as she could. But just as she made it to the corner where an old, abandoned drug store stood she stopped again. Suddenly the file in her arms felt heavy. The cold seeped deeper into her soul. Her mind frantically spammed the rest of her body to keep moving towards home, to stick to the plan. Instead, her feet shuffled over to the stoop of the old drug store, and she sat down first step.

Without warning, her nose began to tingle. The file slipped from her grip and exploded open on the sidewalk as she began to ugly cry. Tears streamed down her face allowing the cold to zap her cheeks even harder. She covered her mouth to muffle her cries, but they still echoed on the storefront. After a while, a growing soreness in her throat forced her to stop. She wiped her nose with her sleeve as she looked up. Some part of her hoped to see some stars but the streetlamps made the sky look pitch black. Her eyes fell back down to the file with its contents strewn everywhere. Work was at eight the next day; she needed to gather everything up and get home soon. This thought ran in her head over and over, but her body stayed where it was. Still, stiff, and waiting to freeze into the night.

Honk!

Tammy's heart jumped at the abrupt sound. She looked around to figure out what made it but saw nothing.

Honk! Honk!

It was closer now. She sat up, alarmed, and took another look around.

"Um, hello? Is someone there?"

As she finished speaking, something from the corner of her eye moved. Making its way around the corner was a clown staring right at her with a bulb horn in hand. His face was painted white with red lips and black diamond eyes. He wore a yellow and red striped costume with a black frilly collar at the neck and was draped in a dirty brown trench coat covered in circus themed pockets. The messy black hair that sprouted from his head went down to his shoulders. He walked towards her slowly before stopping a few feet from where she sat.

Tammy looked at him up and down, completely baffled. Of all the things she thought she was going to appear; this was not one of them. After a moment of silence passed, the clown squeezed the bulb horn again; the resulting honk made her yelp. When her nerves settled down, she faced the disheveled clown and cleared her throat.

"Can I help you?" Her asked with a quivering voice.

The clown tilted his head to the side, looking confused. He tucked the bulb horn away then reached into a pocket with a seal sewn on it and pulled out a bouquet of paper flowers. Tammy stared in disbelief as he handed them to her with a blank expression. Her gut screamed at her to run back to her apartment and lock the door, but her curiosity kept her still. She slowly took the bouquet from him and examined it. The flowers were faded like they had been made years ago and smelled like old books. She looked back at the clown with a nervous smile.

"Uh, t-thank you. They're really nice," she stammered out.

The clown smiled widely. Before she could say or do anything, he sat next to her on the storefront while still allowing some space. He stared at her for a few minutes before using a finger to do a tear motion down his face. At first, she didn't know what he was doing. Then it clicked.

"Oh, this? It's nothing really. I just had a long day," she said as she wiped the tears away.

Even in the echo, she could hear how pathetic she sounded. The clown raised an eyebrow. Tammy tried to hold her face in a half-smile but her resolve soon dissolved and she sighed.

"Well, it's not fine. I guess- it's just-...it's been a long year for me. Well... longer than usual."

The clown blinked and tilted his head again. She thought for a minute then let the flood gates open.

"I just feel so trapped. My life is ruling over me, and I can't do anything but go along with it. My job has taken over everything, I barely see any of my friends and my family is either moving on without me or gone." She paused to take a deep breath. The feeling of the winter air in her lungs was almost refreshing. "I was hoping to get an escape tonight, but it didn't turn out well. I'm all alone. At this point I don't know if it's my fault or the universe is out to get me."

Again, she paused to glance at the clown. He was still there, still listening. She let out a half-hearted laugh before continuing.

"God, I sound like a teenager, don't I? This is the same kind of shit I would say in high school. I'm so pathetic."

A police car passed by, slowing down where they sat, then continued down the vacant street. Tammy looked over to the clown who was searching through his pockets for something. Eventually he pulls out a long, thin red balloon and a pump. He quickly inflated it then twisted it up into sections.

She watched as he made the balloon into the vague shape of a dog. When he was done, he put the pump back in a pocket and presented the balloon dog to her. She couldn't help but laugh.

"That's impressive. You're really good at that...Thank you for trying to cheer me up but I'm afraid it's going to take a lot more than a balloon animal to make me feel better."

The clown's smile fell to an exaggerated frown. He pulled out a pin from one of his pockets and pressed it against the elastic tube, popping it loudly in both of their faces. They sat together quietly, looking out into the empty street. Then, the clown snapped his fingers, stood up, and darted around the corner while Tammy stared after him. When she didn't move, he popped his head back around and motioned for her to follow. Again, a nagging feeling told her to run while she had the chance, but she ignored it and followed him.

When she rounded the corner, she found the clown standing next to a motorcycle. It was clearly old with rust on some of the chrome and its black paint chipping away. Its handlebars had red and yellow ribbons coming out like a child's bicycle and there was a large sack strapped behind the back seat. The clown hopped on the bike and kicked up the stand then gestured for her to join. Tammy barely thought it through before walking over and climbing onto the back-passenger seat, tucking the paper flowers into her coat.

Once she was on, the clown turned the ignition key, its smiley face keychain swung with the sudden motion. Despite the unkempt look of the bike, the engine roared as if it was brand new. In seconds they were off, barreling down the street and running any red light that tried to stop them. Tammy wrapped both arms around the clown's waist in desperation. She wanted to close her eyes but couldn't; the fear of not seeing what was happening was stronger. The clown continued to speed through the city streets, making random turns and dodging bar stragglers along the way.

Soon after their ride began, the red and blue lights of a cop car flashed behind them. Tammy's heart skipped a beat and she clung tighter to the clown. He didn't seem fazed. Instead, she watched as his left hand disappeared into one of his pockets and pulled out a flare. He bit off the paper tip, allowing a blinding red spark to shoot out, then chucked it behind them. Tammy listened as the cop slammed on his brakes and crashed into something. From the sound of gushing water, she guessed it was a fire hydrant. The clown drove on as if nothing happened.

After aimlessly zooming down the streets, the clown slowed down and stopped in front of a thrift store. He turned off the ignition and kicked the stand out, letting Tammy hop off before himself. She watched as he walked right up to the entrance and gave the door a tug, but it refused to budge. He tried again but it stayed in place.

"I-I think it's locked. It's one in the morning so they're not going to be open," Tammy explained.

The clown turned to her, looking puzzled, then raised a finger into the air with a smile. He looked around and spotted a metal trash bin only a few feet away which he rushed over to pick up. From the way his cheeks puffed out, Tammy could tell that it was heavier than he thought it would be. After some shuffling and panting, the clown dragged the trash bin to the entrance. He stopped for a moment to catch his breath then, in one motion, picked up the bin and heaved it towards the doors. The entire thing shattered, and glass rained down like falling crystals.

Tammy held a hand up to her mouth in shock; any alcohol in her system fizzled out as reality came crashing down. The clown kicked in a few leftover shards sticking out before stepping inside. She looked around for anyone who could witness their crime but there was no one. Her eyes then spotted a video camera just above where the glass doors were, its little red light blinking in the darkness. It wouldn't be long before someone looked through the tape and identified her. Everyone will find out and the life that she built will be ruined. Her body tensed up then relaxed as a new thought came to mind and she walked through the broken glass.

By the time she got inside, the clown was raiding the men's section, trying to match shoes up to his feet before tossing them to the side. He hardly seemed to notice she was there, which she didn't mind as she made her way to the women's section. Using her phone for light, she perused the dress section in all its tacky glory, until technicolor sequins caught her eye. She pushed the weird-smelling clothes aside to find a short, spaghetti strapped dress covered in black sequins that sparkled like stars. A smile stretched over her lips. She set her phone on the ground to remove her stuffy office clothes.

To her surprise, the dress slid onto her body with ease, hugging her curves perfectly. She found a pair of short clear heels that fit her well enough and, after some searching, a giant fur coat that smelled of soap. After examining herself in the mirror and teasing her hair to look less like she had been running from the cops, she strolled over to the clown, snagging a small purse as she went. A mountain of shoes sat by the edge of the racks while the clown stood by, reading a paperback upside-down, still wearing his old shoes. As Tammy approached, he looked up. She put on a smile and held out her arms to show off her spur-of-the-moment outfit change.

"What do you think?"

The clown gave her a thumbs up then tossed the book he was reading and headed towards the exit. She paused, slightly miffed from being brushed off, but followed him anyways. By the time she got there, he was already on the bike, ready to go. Without a thought, she hopped onto the back seat. The clown revved the engine and off they went again. As they re-entered the city, Tammy leaned close to his ear.

"So where are we going now?"

The clown didn't respond. His silence began to grate on her nerves.

"Are you ever going to say anything or am I gonna talk to myself all night?"

Again, the clown didn't respond. Tammy looked into the side mirror to see his eyes fixed on the road. She gave up and wrapped her arms around him, resting her head on his back. The cold air froze her legs but for some reason, she felt warm inside. They zoomed back downtown with the same furious speed as before. By now the night shift employees were shuffling to get home while the morning shift shuffled to get into work. The clown paid them no mind as he swerved around the tired zombies. Only one of them was awake enough to curse at them. Tammy responded by flipping them off. Two more turns in the route and she spotted a familiar logo.

"Hey, can we stop here?"

The clown nodded and pulled over by the sidewalk. Before the bike came to a stop, Tammy jumped off, her eyes tracing the company sign she's seen every morning for the last five years. Sleek, modern, and so generic it was painful. She tried to remember her first day, younger and beaming with pride that she could get a job right after college. That seemed like a lifetime ago. The clown walked up next to her, following her gaze upward. She laughed dryly.

"I can't tell you how much crap I put up with here. I tried to apply for other jobs, but no one wanted me. So, I just...gave up. Why bother if the world doesn't want you?"

From the corner of her eye, she noticed the clown nod his head slightly. She smiled.

"Tomorrow I have to be here at eight and I probably won't get out until seven or eight. It's been that way for the last year. Do you have anything that can fix that?"

The clown brought his thumb to his chin as he pondered then snapped his fingers. He ran back to his bike and opened the sack behind the passenger seat. Tammy tip toed behind him to see what he was doing. Before she could get a closer look, a bundle of dynamite was shoved into her face. There were four sticks wrapped up in a comically long primer cord. She looked at the clown in disbelief while he grinned devilishly.

"Don't you think that's a little excessive? The blast might hurt us too," she pointed out. Then she looked up at the logo again, its irritating light made her eye twitch. "Do you think we'll be fast enough?"

She got an enthusiastic nod in response. Now it was her turn to ponder their next move. It didn't take long for her to return the grin. The clown handed her the end of the primer cord then ran up the steps, unraveling the dynamite as he went. To both of their surprise, there was a little bit of cord left once he got to the doors. Once he set the dynamite down, he sprinted back to her. Tammy handed him the end of the cord while he searched his pockets. Soon he pulled out a lighter and, after clicking it a few times, held the end of the cord to the flame.

It burned brightly as he dropped it on the ground and traveled up the line like a sparkler. The two of them jumped onto the bike and roared away without looking back. For a moment, only the wind whistled through Tammy's ears. Then she heard a tremendous boom along with creaking metal and shattering glass. Some giggles slipped past her lips before she threw her head back and started cackling so loud it echoed down the streets. In her euphoria, she thought she heard the clown chuckling as well but when she stopped to listen, she heard nothing. Soon emergency sirens blared between the skyscrapers and her panic returned.

"Let's get out of here!" She gasped.

With a nod, the clown took the next turn and zoomed down the road out of the city. They traveled past many boarded up houses and liquor shops before the sirens finally died down. Tammy rested her head on the clown's back, eyes closed and listening to the purr of the engine. In her moment of peace, she heard another motorcycle coming from behind them. She tried to ignore it, but it grew louder and closer until she finally opened her eyes. There, another clown rode next to them, and she almost yelped in surprise. This one was much bigger, wearing a white and black striped costume and a little white cone hat on his head. He looked over to Tammy and she turned away.

Then another bike appeared on the other side of them. The driver was a lanky clown in hobo clothes while the passenger was a shorter clown in red hula-hoop pants and a fluffy blue wig. Gradually, more bikes showed up with clowns of all shapes, sizes, and colors. None of them spoke a word and all of them kept their eyes locked on the road. Occasionally, one would glance at Tammy for a second before looking away. She hugged her clown even tighter as she followed their eyes to where they were going.

Just beyond the last rundown house was a tree line she didn't notice before where a golden glow arose. The gang of clowns drove off the road and into the woods, somehow gliding through the foliage while staying close. The glow grew brighter with deeper shades of orange as the separate flames of a fire began to stand out. Then the trees parted into a clearing where a giant pile of burning wood was in the center. The clowns circled around it a few times before going off to the clearing's edge to park their bikes. Tammy held on as her clown stopped next to a bike with twin clown girls then nudged her to move. As soon as they were both off, she looked him up and down, not sure what to say until it dawned on her.

"What's your name?"

Her clown's face brightened. Without a word, he gave her a quick wink. He did this a few more times before she came up with a guess.

"Winky? Is that your name?"

Her clown shrugged while giving her a goofy smile. Tammy smiled.

"Alright, I'll call you Winky then."

He bowed and held out a hand to her. She raised an eyebrow before taking it. By now, the clowns were gathering around the bonfire, shouting and yelling gibberish while they danced. One of them pulled out an accordion and started to play. Others joined him with their own instruments as they formed a shoe-string band. They played a wacky song while the rest either paired off or danced in a circle. Tammy was soon separated from Winky but didn't mind. One of the groups took her in and she soon found herself dancing.

Around the blazing fire she danced and laughed along with the colorful company. At some point, her heels and coat fell off, but she didn't care. Even when the cold ground made her toes numb, she continued to party like never before. Between the breaks of people, she spotted Winky sitting along the edge next to an old woman wearing a long patchwork cloak. He was whispering something into her ear, and she nodded. Tammy tried to break free to join them but was dragged back in by the crowd.

After hours of dancing from one crazy tune to the next, she finally stopped to sit by the fire. She had just warmed the tips of her fingers when the joyful music suddenly stopped, and the mood went solum out of nowhere. She turned around to see what was going on. All the clowns were facing the elderly woman outside the circle with Winky and the bigger clown in stripes by her side. To Tammy's horror, the striped clown held an ax with an absurdly large blade.

Her fear grew when both clowns made their way towards her while the others moved aside to let them through. The urge to run shot through her body and she stood up to back away. Some of the clowns blocked her path, gently grabbing her arms and giving her reassuring smiles. The striped clown marched right up to her then stopped a few feet away. He lifted the ax up high then paused as if he was waiting for something while Winky trotted up to his side. Tammy's eyes darted between the two of them; her mind buzzing with questions.

Then Winky pinched the end of his frilly collar and pulled down, revealing a nasty cut that was crudely stitched up around his neck. Tammy stared in shock, not sure what he was trying to say. Then a waving hand caught her attention. It was the hobo clown with his collar pulled down, showing a similar wound and stitch pattern. In every direction she looked, the clowns tugged at their collars to expose their sewn-up necks. The gears turned in her head as she looked up to the striped clown, who had completely removed his collar for her to see his stitches. She blinked a few more times then took a deep breath.

"Okay, I think I get it," she muttered.

She shook off the hands that held her and calmly approached him. With one last glance to Winky, she got down on one knee and pulled her hair out of the way. The striped clown took the cue, bringing the ax down to make a clean cut. Her head rolled away while Tammy's body collapsed onto the ground. A tremendous cheer erupted from the crowd as Winky scuttled over to retrieve the head. Five clowns stepped forward to pick up the body and marched over to the old woman, who was busy sewing a dress by hand. She watched as the body was laid in front of her with Winky following, Tammy's head in his hands. The woman set the dress aside and looked at the content face of the recently deceased girl.

"She's very beautiful," she remarked, "And spunky from what I've seen. She'll make a lovely new friend."

She took the head in her hands and placed it in her lap. Then she reached into her cloak to pull out a long needle and a spool of black thread and set to work. With careful precision, she pierced the needle close to the edge of the neck then connected it to the stump on the body. Over and over, she drew her needle in a crisscross pattern around the wound, all the while humming a melody only she knew. The clowns surrounding her watched in anticipation. Beyond the blazing flames of the fire the dark sky shifted to a rich navy blue. The old woman paused her work to stick her nose up, taking a deep breath. Winky looked at her perplexed and scooted closer.

"I'm just taking in the morning air child, don't rush me," she said, "I have plenty of time."

She returned to her work, finishing the last few stitches before knotting up the end. A pair of scissors was pulled from her cloak to snip away the excess thread. Then she placed a hand on each side of the girl's head and closed her eyes.

"Any minute now," she whispered.

The crowd of clowns leaned closer in bated breath. For several minutes, nothing happened. The sky slowly changed to a lighter shade of blue with hints of orange and pink coming from the East. Then a toe on Tammy's foot twitched, then a few fingers, then her nose flared. Her eyes scrunched up tightly before fluttering open.

"There you are sunshine," the woman mused, "Welcome back."

The crowd applauded as Tammy sat up and Winky scooted right up to her. The sky was now painted in bright yellow and orange. The bonfire slowly disappeared and one by one, the clowns vanished as the sun's rays reached further into their dark shelter. Tammy looked around confused.

"I'm afraid we don't have enough time to give you a new name, my dear. We must go now," the old woman explained, "But tomorrow I should have your clothes ready, and we'll get everything sorted out. Is that alright?"

Tammy thought for a moment then nodded. The sun peeked up over the trees and they too disappeared.

Brand New Thing

[Hey. You up?]

Alan stared at the text message that just popped up on his screen. He was tempted to lay down and finally get back to bed like he was supposed to, but his profile was showing him active so she wouldn't have bought that excuse. He sighed then typed.

[Yeah, but I need to get to bed soon.]

[Dude. I just discovered something. I need you to sit on the floor and meditate.]

[Julia, I need to get to sleep. I have an exam tomorrow.]

[It'll only take a few minutes.]

Again, Alan sighed. He could argue but knew it wasn't going to get him anywhere. She was gonna pester him until three in the morning if he tried to ignore her. With a grunt, he slid off the bed and sat down on the floor, legs crossed.

[Alright. I'm doing it.]

[OK. Count down from three then think about a green apple and hold onto that image.]

He looked up at the time before locking his phone and setting it aside. After taking a deep breath, he began to count.

3...2...1

The image of a green apple immediately popped into his head. He focused in on its smooth skin and round shape; his stomach growled a little just looking at it. As he continued to focus, he noticed that his breath felt a little lighter. Like he was breathing in early spring air. Then, he started to hear a faint breeze blowing through trees. He wanted to open his eyes but reasoned against it.

I'm just imagining things.

He continued to focus on the apple until the sound of an orchestra started up in the distance followed by the laughter of children. Then came the chirping birds and buzzing of flies. He turned his head side to side in disbelief. When he felt the ground under him shift, he finally opened his eyes to see what was going on. A bright light nearly blinded him, sunlight. He blinked a few times to ease the strain.

When his vision finally came back into focus, the first thing he saw was a tree growing giant green apples slightly bigger than someone's head. His eyes widened and his jaw dropped. Before he could comprehend what was happening, two flashes of color zoomed past him. They were two boys wearing the most vibrant, outdated clothes he'd ever seen. The scent of tulips slowly crept up to his nose as he finally stood up to look around.

There were people sitting on emerald grass; talking, walking around the few statues sprinkled around the green, or gathering around one of the groups performing music. It was like a scene from an old cartoon. Alan looked around frantically, wondering how he got to such a place. Then, he spotted her staring at him from atop a hill. Her curly red hair tied back and wearing an oversized band t-shirt with basketball shorts. She sat cross-legged and smiled at him warmly.

"Julia?" He muttered.

Immediately, he started to sprint towards her. Not four steps in, he crashed into something and fell back. When he looked up again, he was back in his room, no green field, no children, no music. His attention was caught by a small ding from his phone. It was a message from Julia of only a laughing-until-crying emoji. He snatched it up and started typing.

[What the hell was that?!]

[Pepperland. I took us there using astral projection.]

[Huh? What are you talking about?]

[I'll explain tomorrow. You should get some sleep before your exam. ;)]

He was about to start typing but stopped. She wasn't going to say any more that night and he knew it; she liked keeping him curious. Instead, he reassured his roommate that knocked on his door that he was fine and climbed back into bed, his head still throbbing.

Morning Routine

A strong wind rattled the window as a little girl slept soundly in her bed. Her blankets were wrapped around her body as if she were a burrito while the numerous stuffed animals around her stood watch. She had just turned in her sleep when her bedroom door cracked open. Blood-red eyes peered into the room, focusing on her sleeping frame. A long, clawed hand gently pushed open the door and a shadowy figure crept inside. It stepped over the toys and book strewn on the floor and soon made it to the edge of the bed, hovering over the girl. Then, with its monstrous hands, it reached out to grab her tiny shoulder and gave it a shake.

"Emma. It's time to get up," a deep voice whispered.

The girl turned to face away from the figure while pulling the covers over her head.

"Emma," the figure said a little louder, "It's time for you to go to school."

Emma remained still, hoping to get away with pretending to not hear the voice. However, another good shake of the shoulder let her know that he was not buying it. She fumbled to sit on her bed, the blanket still wrapped around her, then opened her groggy eyes.

"I'm up Uncle Nos," she muttered.

"Very good. Get yourself dressed. I made breakfast."

With that, the figure slipped out of the room just before the first sliver of morning light peeked through the curtains. Emma let out a big yawn before wrestling the blankets from her body and swinging her feet over the side of the bed. She shuffled over to the vanity mirror where her school uniform had been laid out the night before and flipped the switch. The light from the bulbs stung but she bore it just enough to change clothes and brush out her hair. Next, she went into the bathroom to brush her teeth then pattered down the stairs to the kitchen.

The blinds on all the windows had been pulled down to block out any sunlight and a dozen candles on the kitchen counter were all lit. Standing by the counter was a tall, pale man with a bald head and pointy ears. He set a plate of pancakes in front of the chair Emma usually took next to her waiting backpack.

"Did you sleep well?" He asked in his usual monotone voice.

"Yeah, I slept okay," Emma replied as she slid into her seat.

"Are you ready for your math test today?"

"As ready as I can be, I guess."

He nodded then went over to the coffee maker that had finished making a fresh pot.

"Hey Uncle Nos, I think I heard a sound outside my window last night," Emma said while cutting the pancakes.

"Oh? What kind of sound?"

"I don't know. Like something was climbing through the trees then landed on our roof. It sounded really big."

"Hm. Perhaps it was one of the stray cats."

"No no! Something bigger! Like a person!"

"Now my dear, I would have noticed if a person was trying to break into our home from the roof. You may be misremembering."

Emma opened her mouth to argue but his blank expression told her that it probably wouldn't be worth it. She sighed then continued to eat her breakfast in silence while he poured himself a cup of coffee and took a sip.

"Ah! Perfect," he muttered to himself.

Suddenly, the phone sitting by the stove buzzed. He sat his mug down to reach over and tap the screen.

"Ah, it seems Ashley's mom is here to pick you up," he said.

"Hold on!"

Emma scarfed down the last of the pancakes before quickly wiping her face and grabbing her backpack.

"You have swim practice tonight. Did you remember to pack your swimsuit?"

"Yeah, I got it!"

"And did you remember to pack that overdue book to return? I don't want to get another email from the school library."

"I remembered!"

She ran over to the front door to slip on her shoes. Before grabbing the door handle, she looked back to the man standing in the kitchen archway, mug in hand.

"I'll see you tonight, Uncle Nos!" She said with a smile before slipping outside.

He nodded behind her, listening as her footsteps got farther and farther away. When he finally heard a minivan pull away, he calmly ascended the stairs and glided down the hall towards the linen closet. As soon as he pulled the door open, the body of a vampire hunter spilled out; his long coat covered in crosses and stinking of garlic. His neck had been twisted in an awkward angle while his eyes were frozen in terror. Nos took another sip of his coffee as he examined the body.

"Now what am I going to do with you?" he pondered out loud.

Campfire Stories

"We are so getting kicked out of here."

The three other friends laughed around the campfire while some clothes sat on the cold dirt in front of a modest pile of beer cans. Jen looked around at them then took a swig from her mostly full bottle of Jack Daniels. Dan leaned back on a log by himself, beer in hand, flushed and chuckling. Eric sat on another log with his fiancée Katie leaning on him, beyond buzzed. She giggled at Jen's comment.

"What the park rangers don't know won't hurt them," she slurred in response, "Besides, it's not like anyone's going to see him."

"Unless he gets lost," Dan remarked, "We'll probably get into more trouble if we're caught this far out from the official campsite."

"I don't think anyone would blame us for moving away from that troop of cub scouts, though," Eric said.

Jen shrugged and took another swig.

"Knowing him, he's gonna run out onto the main road before he gets back," Eric said.

"Or get kicked in the balls by a moose," Jen suggested.

Katie giggled. Eric pulled her closer to keep her warm and she nuzzled into his body with a smile. Jen rolled her eyes while she suppressed a chuckle.

"So, who's next?" Dan asked.

"I think it's Jen's turn since she dared Ben," Eric said.

"How about no. This is getting boring," Jen retorted.

"Agreed," Katie piped up.

The two guys looked at each other, silently debating if it was worth arguing, then shrugged.

"Alright, let's do something else," Dan said as he grabbed another beer, "What are we doing now?"

They heard loud footsteps from the dark forest running towards them. Out of the bushes, Ben sprinted into the campsite, buck naked and panting. Eric and Dan burst into a fit of laughter as he jogged over to his clothes.

"Holy shit I got so close to getting caught!" He gasped, pulling on his boxers, "I thought the rangers only stuck around during the day."

"You know you could have just done the two truths," Jen pointed out.

"Fuck that, I'm not a pussy!"

"Just stupid," Eric mumbled.

Ben put on the rest of his clothes before returning to his seat next to Dan. He reached for a beer in the cooler and opened it.

"So, who's next?" he asked as he took a sip.

"We're moving on to something else," Jen answered.

"Huh? Why? We were just getting started!" Ben whined.

"Waiting around for someone to do their dare is getting boring," she explained.

"Yeah, I'm not in the mood for getting naked," Dan said.

Ben's expression dropped and he slumped over his beer.

"Killjoys," he muttered.

"Besides, some of us are getting a little too tipsy to be doing stupid stuff in the woods," Eric added, not bothering to hide his accusing finger pointed at the girl under his arm. It took Katie a minute to realize who he was talking about.

"I'm not drunk!" She spouted.

"Oh yeah? How many fingers am I holding up?"

Eric held up three fingers then slowly moved his hand around in different directions. Katie tried to follow, then her dizzy eyes fixed on him as best as she could.

"Fuck you," she spat.

Eric laughed. Jen looked on.

"Well, what are we doing then?" Ben blurted out.

"Why don't we tell ghost stories?" Jen suggested.

"That sounds fun!" Katie said.

"Lame!" Ben shouted.

"Oh, I'm sorry. I didn't know we had a pussy with us tonight," Jen retorted.

"You say what now?"

"Alright, it's decided! We're telling ghost stories!" Eric announced.

The group fell silent as each of them tried to think of a good tale to tell. A cool wind gently blew by, making them all shiver. Eric grabbed his jacket on the ground and wrapped it around Katie.

"I think I got one," Dan said, "Though it's been a while since I heard it so, I don't remember it word for word."

"Go ahead," Eric said.

"Okay. So, there was this poor guy who worked as a handy man. One day, a rich oil tycoon called him about fixing up an old mansion in the next town over. The handyman had heard rumors about the place, but the oil tycoon promised a big payment that would help him get out of debt. When he gets to the mansion, he gets an overall weird vibe about it. It was big but rundown. Windows were cracked or completely broken, the walls looked like they were about to collapse, and the lawn was overgrown with weeds. The whole nine yards. While he checked out the property, the handyman felt like he was being watch by invisible eyes.

"Regardless, he goes into the mansion alone with nothing but his toolbox. He decides to first give the house a full inspection before he did anything. He went from room to room, starting from the top floor and worked his way down. As he went through the motions, he couldn't shake the feeling that he was being watched. Finally, when the initial inspection was nearly complete, he went to the basement door to check out the water boiler and pipes. The moment he opened it, he felt lightheaded and his heart started to race. From the edge of his senses, he thought he heard horrified screams. He slammed the door shut, grabbed his toolbox, and ran out of the mansion. But when he tried to start his truck to leave, it stalled. He tried and tried again but it refused to start. Desperate to leave, the handyman got out of the truck and ran for the large open gates out of the property. Just as he was about to pass through to freedom, he heard a small voice call to him:

"Don't go."

"How much longer is this story?" Ben whined.

Three shushes made him shrink back in his seat. Dan waited for any other interruptions before continuing.

"Anyways, the handyman sprinted towards the town and into the first bar that was open. He tried to tell anyone who would listen about what he experienced but no one would even look at him. Eventually, the bartender handed him a beer and sat him down at the end of the bar. He explained that no one goes inside the old mansion because anyone who entered it suffered great misfortune. The handyman listened and decided to tell the tycoon he would no longer work for him. Then he remembered that his truck and his toolbox were still parked in the mansion driveway. The bartender tried to talk him out of going back but without a toolbox or truck, the handyman would lose his job. After some back and forth, the bartender agreed to drive him back to the mansion and jumpstart his truck.

"By the time they left the bar, it was dark. They drove to the mansion and jumped the truck back to life. They were about to leave when the handyman noticed that his toolbox was gone. The bartender begged him to leave it, even promised to give him a used one, but the handyman insisted. They decided to go inside together, thinking they would at least have each other. When they entered, they saw that the basement door was wide open. The handyman told the bartender that he had closed it before he left. They knew they had to get out but the anxious feeling the handyman felt before was gone. With some convincing, the handyman and the bartender descended into the basement to look for the toolbox.

"The next morning, the bar wasn't open. The patrons told the police about the night before and they went to investigate. When they got there, they found the bartender's car and the truck; both dead. Then officers went into the mansion to search for the men.... It was never released what they found that day. Anyone who tries to ask them about it only got shrugs. As far as the police or townspeople will say, no one went to the mansion that night."

The awed silence after the story's completion was broken by Eric.

"That was a good one."

Ben drank his beer quietly as Dan took in the praise. Katie snuggled closer to Eric while Jen stared into the fire then took another swig of liquor.

"I think I heard something similar to that in summer camp," she remarked once her throat was clear.

"It was something my dad told me once. He said it was a campfire story when he was younger," Dan explained.

The clank of an empty beer can thrown into the trash pile made all of them jump in their seats. Jen felt a shiver go up her spine but kept calm.

"I think I have our next story," she said after another drink from her bottle.

"Go for it," Eric encouraged.

Ben looked into his beer can.

"I've only heard this story once so don't shit on me too hard," Jen prefaced, then took a swig. "A long time ago, there was a beautiful girl who lived with her farmer father. While she had several suitors, her father refused to give away her hand in marriage because he felt that none of the boys in the village were good enough for her. One day, while she was out milking the cows, she noticed a shadowy figure watching her at the edge of the forest. When she turned to see who it was, the figure was gone. For the next week she would constantly catch glimpses of it while she did her chores. She tried to tell her father about it but he dismissed it as girlish paranoia-"

"Sounds like he needs to get woke!" Ben exclaimed randomly.

A death glare from Jen and the groans of the rest of the audience forced him to again sink back in his seat. Another beer can hit the pile.

"Anyways. While the daughter kept seeing the shadowy figure, the farmer noticed things happening on the farm while his back was turned. The broken fence by the chicken coop was mended, a hole in the roof of the barn was fixed, and the squeaking hinge of the front door was oiled. At first, he wrote it off as his neighbor helping him out. Then one night, just as he was on the brink of slumber, he heard a ghostly whisper in his ear:

'Farmer, I would like to take your daughter as my wife. As you can see, I am a perfect fit as a husband and can provide for her every need. All I ask is your blessing.'

"The farmer jumped out of his sleep, a cold sweat forming on his brow. He questioned his sanity, obviously, then lay his head back down to rest. This went on for three nights. On the morning of the fourth day, his daughter came to him with a pale face.

"'Father, I've been hearing a whisper in my ear while I sleep. It tells me that it loves me and it wants to take me away to be its wife. It tells me about how it longs to kiss me and have me bear its children.'"

"Now the farmer was afraid. The thought occurred to him that the voice he heard was a demon. Within an hour he had his daughter sent away to a relative's home then sent for a pastor to exorcise his land. They blessed every corner of his property from the garden to the fields where the horses grazed. That night he lay his head on his pillow and listened. When he heard nothing-"

"I'm getting bored!" Katie slurred.

Eric gently squeezed her body, causing her to let out a small yelp before giggling. Jen paused and watched the two snicker. A breeze brushed the back of her neck and the shrubs behind her rustled. She looked over to Dan who met her gaze and shrugged. Off to the side, Ben stared at his phone. Eventually, Eric looked up.

"Well, what happens next?" He asked.

A cough forced its way out of Jen's throat. She took a moment to have a drink then continued.

"The next day, the farmer went to fetch his daughter. They were excited to return to a home that was now demon free. For a little while, everything was fine. However, when they had their lunch one day, the farmer got an uneasy feeling. Like someone was glaring into the back of his head. He looked to his daughter to see if she felt it but she seemed carefree as always. That night, as he lay in bed about to drift off to sleep, he heard a shuffling noise above him. He opened his eyes and looked up.

"A tall, shadowy figure loomed over him. Its thin mouth twisted into a snarl while its blood-red eyes glared at him. Outside his bedroom door, he could hear his daughter scream for help. The farmer tried to get up, but his body wouldn't move. Even his fingers refused to curl into fists. All he could do was lay there under the horrifying creature until his eyelids betrayed him. The next morning, he was woken by the chirping of the birds. He flung out of bed and charged towards his daughter's room, but she wasn't there, and she was never found again."

The fire popped a few times in the brief silence after Jen finished. Dan and Eric nodded in approval while Katie continued to slouch.

"Nice," Eric said.

Jen smiled then took another drink. There was about a third of the bottle left.

"Yeah, reeeally scary," Ben sneered, "Gonna soil my undies from that one."

Some laughs followed. Jen looked for the source but the everyone was straight-faced. She then turned to Ben.

"Well then, smart ass, why don't you tell us a story?" She said with a smirk.

Ben's eyes widened.

"What? ME? No, I couldn't!"

"Dude, you interrupted both me and Jen when it was our turn," Dan pointed out, "It's only fair."

"Oh come on! You all know I was joking."

"All in favor of Ben telling a story, say 'aye'," Eric said.

"Aye." "Aye." "Aye!"

Ben looked around for someone to defend him, but four pairs of eyes stared back at him in mild anticipation. Another empty beer can crashed into the pile. Finally, Ben sighed in defeat.

"Fine!" He sputtered, "But no one interrupt me!"

Jen and Dan caught each other's glance then rolled their eyes. Dan reached into the cooler but stopped and looked inside with a quizzical look. After counting on his hand a few times, he shrugged and pulled out a new can.

"Throw me one dude!" Ben begged.

A full can was chucked at him which he caught right before it hit him in the nose. He cracked it open, chugged it, then wiped the foam off his lip.

"Alright! So, in this forest out west there's an area that's rumored to be home to a monster. It hides in the trees and shadows but can sometimes appear during the day. It hunts for children who wander off from the playground and will gladly slaughter any adult who comes looking for them. They say that if you go out at night and steal eight magic pages from its lair it will disappear, but no one has ever come out of those woods alive. Oooo!"

He stretched his arms out, wiggling his fingers for effect, only to be met with blank stares.

"Dude, that's Slenderman," Jen bluntly said.

"What? No it's not!" Ben defended, "I made that up on the spot."

"Yes it is."

"It's not!"

"Dude, I don't give a shit about internet stuff and even I know that's Slenderman," Dan added in.

"Oh fuck off!"

"Dude, calm down. You're acting like an ass," Eric said.

For a brief second, Ben's face puffed up, red as a beet, then slumped back muttering a bitter "whatever". An uncomfortable silence fell on the group as they waited for someone to speak up. But Dan and Jen kept sipping on their drinks while Ben pulled out his phone again. An empty can hitting the pile spooked them.

"So, are we done?" Eric asked.

"But we just got started," Jen pointed out.

"Yeah, but it is getting a little late," Dan mentioned.

"And someone here is close to falling asleep," Eric said, nudging the girl under his arm.

Katie blinked twice and looked around.

"I'm fine," she sighed, "I'm just- I'm just resting my head."

A hiccup escaped her lips, causing Eric to bust out laughing. A few more chuckles joined in. The bushes rustled again but was ignored by the group. Jen took another swig only to realize there was only half a sip left. She stared at the bottle then tossed it aside.

"Well, if we're in the mood for one more story, I think I have our last tale," Eric offered.

"Fine by me," Dan yawned.

Jen remained quiet while Ben stared off into the woods.

"This is actually a story that the park ranger told me when we were checking in," Eric prefaced. He took a last gulp of his lukewarm beer before he began, "About fifty years ago, there was this house owned by a strange family called the Jones, around the edge of town. The father was a handyman who took work where he could get it and the mother was a typical housewife. They had a few children but none of them wandered far from their own backyard. Overall, the town considered them to be a relatively normal family. Over time, however, the townspeople started noticing that drifters were going missing. Homeless men who used to commune in the alleys were disappearing.

"At first, this was considered a good change; even the mayor commented about it. It wasn't until folks living on the edge of town started going missing that people got worried. All the while, they noticed that Mr. Jones was getting fatter before their eyes, but Mrs. Jones wasn't making her regular trips to the grocery store. Suspicion turned into rumors which turned into serious considerations by the local police. Then one Sunday, the pastor and his wife failed to make it to services. The last person to ever speak to them was Mr. Jones. A mob formed that headed straight for the Jones' home. When they kicked open the front door, they found a horror show.

"The fridge was stuffed with neatly carved portions of human flesh. There were strange sculptures made of bone and dried out skin in the basement. Finally, in the shed, they found the pastor's wife strung up like a deer and decapitated. While there was evidence all around the house, no one could find any trace of the family. A manhunt had formed but it was no use, they were never found. They say that the family is still out there, still looking for local campers to prey on."

The campfire crackled again as the logs collapsed. There was total silence all around the circle, even the forest seemed to quiet down. Eric took one last drink of his beer before throwing his can into the pile. Dan cleared his throat.

".... Dude...."

"Hm?" Eric hummed.

"Is that- Is that seriously what the ranger told you?"

"Well, he gave me the basic gist. They had these old newspaper clippings framed in the office. There were some freaky pictures so I had to ask. I filled in the details for dramatic purposes."

"Wait! You mean the story is real!" Katie squeaked.

Her panicked eyes searched Eric's face for any scrap of falsehood but got nothing. She pushed him away to sit up by her lone, drunken self.

"Eric! How am I supposed to sleep tonight? I fucking hate you!"

The guys laughed as she shuffled her way over to where Jen sat. Eric reached into the cooler but got a strange look on his face.

"Um, who took the last beer?" He asked.

"Don't look at me, I brought my own drink," Jen answered.

The focus soon went to Dan and Ben.

"There were, like, three beers left when I got mine," Dan explained.

"How much did you guys drink?" Eric asked.

Both guys thought for a minute but lacked answers. Eric sighed.

"Forget it, we'll figure it out in the morning," he said.

"Jen, can you help me get to the tent? I can't see in the dark very well," Katie pleaded.

"Yeah, hang on," Jen replied.

After wrapping Katie's arm over her shoulder, she stood up and they wobbled their way over to their tent. The guys continued to stick around the dwindling fire; Eric and Dan chatting about something while Ben sulked. Jen crawled into the tent and Katie immediately collapsed on her sleeping bag.

"Nnnnn, I think I had too much," she moaned.

"Ya think?" Jen laughed.

"How can you even drink a full bottle of whiskey? I can't even have a shot."

"Meh, it gets a good buzz going."

Jen helped pull her boots off and tossed them into the corner of the tent. Katie was already nodding to sleep by the time she was tucked into her bag. Before turning in herself, Jen sat still for a moment then gave Katie a slight nudge.

"Hey, thanks for sleeping here with me. I know you probably wanted to be with Eric but I really didn't want to sleep with the other two," she whispered.

"You're good," Katie mumbled, "It's what friends are for."

A smile stretched on Jen's face as she crawled into her own bag. She rolled around for a short time, trying to get comfortable on the hard ground. After what felt like hours, she found a good divot to place her hip to get into a decent position. Just as she was about to drift off to sleep, she jolted awake. The whiskey finally took effect as her surroundings felt fuzzier. She sat up to look out their tent. The fire looked like it had been started back up but she couldn't hear the boys. She took a few minutes to listen but gave up and rested her head back on her lumpy pillow. Not long after, she was woken up again, this time by a sharp kick. On the other side of the tent, she heard shuffling sounds along with the noise of fleshy smacking. Jen held back a groan as she tried to remain still and pretend not to hear it. Two more nudges from a foot finally made her snap. She turned over to see a large figure on top of Katie, making short, slow movements.

"Seriously Eric? You couldn't wait until we got home to fuck? She's not even going to be able to do anything," she scolded, "Get out! I'm trying to sleep here."

The figure stopped then straightened up to look at her. The fire outside had died down, preventing her from seeing his expression. Her eyes went from the man in front of her to Katie, who was motionless. Then, he crawled his way over to her. The sudden action startled her. She tried to move but he was soon on top of her, straddling her. Jen stared at him in confusion.

"What are you doing?" She whispered.

No response, just breathing.

"Are you actually drunk now?"

Again, no response. He got closer to her, his breathing getting heavier. A strange tingling feeling started in Jen's stomach. When he got right in her face, she leaned forward to give him a sloppy kiss. She felt him immediately stiffened up, but she continued to suck on his lips and grind onto him. After some time, he pulled away and sat in front of her, dazed. It took Jen a few moments to realize what she had done, and her stomach turned. She looked away towards the corner of the tent.

"I- I'm sorry. It's just that I-" the words clogged up in her throat and her nose started to feel prickly as tears formed in her eyes, "I know it's been years but I- I just never could get over you. I...still love you. I know I need to stop but I can't. I still want you."

With the words out, she looked back at him. The atmosphere of the tent felt strange. Then, without saying anything, he crawled through the flimsy flaps into the night. The air went stale as Jen stayed sitting up. Tears started to fall as the gravity of what she had done hit her. She looked over to Katie, who was still sleeping, then laid back down, silently crying until she finally fell asleep. The next thing she knew, it was light out. Fresh dew made everything smell like rain and the birds already began chirping. A massive headache started to form the more conscious she became. There was only one thing on her mind: damage control. The sleeping bag next to her was still quiet. Biting her lip, Jen reached over to give her friend a light shake on the shoulder.

"K-Katie, are you up?" She whispered.

No response. Jen shook her a little harder.

"Katie, I-I know that looked really bad last night. Can we talk about it?"

Still nothing. Her heart dropped.

"Listen, I don't know what you saw but please let me explain," Jen said as she yanked the sleeping bag open.

The color red filled her vision while her nose was assaulted by the pungent smell of copper. There was Katie, covered in her own blood with her intestines spilling out and eyes wide open. A cold shock traveled through Jen's body as her hangover immediately went away.

"Katie?"

The body didn't move. Shaking, Jen reached over to touch her neck. The skin was slightly warm but there was no pulse. Finally, a scream came out of Jen's throat. She fumbled as she kicked her sleeping bag away and frantically crawled out of the tent.

"Eric! Dan! Ben! Help!" She shrieked.

As soon as she broke out of the tent, she stopped. Blood and body parts were strewn around the ash pile that was the campfire. Dan was propped up on a log, his arms and legs removed while his rib cage was torn open. Off to the side, Ben was tied to a tree and was clearly used as a target for knife throwing. His limbs were gone too. Then a little red drop landed on Jen's shoulder, and she froze. Looking up, she saw intestines hung up in the trees like macabre Christmas lights. The sight made her bent forward and vomit. She puked out what felt like a gallon then spotted something only a few yards away. Something roundish but not spherical. She squinted at it then recoiled. Eric's severed head was facing her, staring blankly ahead. Another bloodcurdling scream escaped her throat and she almost fell to her knees.

"Howdy!"

Jen yelped and whipped around to see a man standing behind her with a cartoonish smile on his face. He wore a dirty camo shirt and jeans with a baseball bat resting on his shoulder. A million things went through Jen's mind and none of them were good. The man stood patiently, as if waiting for her to say something, then spoke.

"Lovely morning, huh?" He said.

The words sounded like gibberish. Jen couldn't say anything, so he continued.

"You're a heavy sleeper. We were having all sorts of fun out here. It's not often that we get campers this far out. Most people stick closer to the ranger's office," he prattled on, "My name's Roy by the way."

He held out a hand to shake. Jen just stared at his grinning face.

"You did this?" She whimpered.

Roy nodded as he pulled his arm away.

"Yep! Got some good rations out of it too," he cheerfully said.

The urge to puke came back but she had nothing left in her stomach. She wanted to run but her feet remained planted.

"Did feel a little bad about it though," Roy continued, "Y'all were really good story tellers. Buddy wanted to join in, but it would just be weird, ya know? I liked that guy's the best, no offense," he pointed the bat towards Dan's body, "Love a good, haunted house story. Sorry about stealing your beer by the way. We forgot our canteens."

".....B-Buddy?"

"Oh yeah! He loves campfire stories. You should have seen his face when he got out of your tent. He looked tickled pink. By the way, what happened in there?"

His words didn't register at first. Then Jen's stomach tightened as she brought a hand to her lips. Roy looked at her confused until a light bulb went off in his head.

"Ah! I see. Cheeky little bastard," he chuckled, "No wonder he wanted to keep you alive. Well, how about ya come on back with us! We're gonna have a barbeque with the family tonight so you'll get to meet everyone. We're not the Jones, though. Sorry to disappoint."

The shock that went through Jen's body finally loosened up her legs. She started to back away slowly, her head shaking violently. Roy continued to smile as he stepped towards her.

"Aw, come on now. You don't think we're just gonna let you go after all this, do ya? Besides, ma's been wantin' another set of hands to help out around the house."

Just as she was about to turn and run, she backed into something big. She looked up to find herself in the chest of a man around Eric's build wearing a mechanic's jumpsuit. He stared down at her, his blue eyes piercing into her soul and gave her a large grin, exposing his yellow crooked teeth. She froze. Emotions crashed around in her mind, drowning her. She grew dizzy and her vision blurred. As she staggered away, Buddy's smile turned into a look of concern.

"Oh, hold on there, darlin'!" Roy cried out.

Jen dropped hard on the dirt ground, feeling nothing as the world slowly dissolved into black.

The Talk

The dining table was abnormally quiet as the Bailey family ate their meatloaf dinner. At first, Harvey Bailey paid no mind to the silence since he had just arrived home from a long day of boardroom meetings discussing the latest line of service robots he was expected to prototype. But he got the feeling that something was amiss and looked up to see his wife Martha giving him a concerned glance. She motioned over to their son David, who was picking away at his peas. That's when he realized that the boy hadn't said a word since they sat down.

By this point in the evening, David would be prattling on about the latest science fact his teacher told him or an argument he had with his friend Tommy on the playground. But tonight, he sat in his chair quietly with melancholic expression on his face. Even when Harvey arrived home, he found him filling out his multiplication tables without complaint. Clearly, something was bothering the boy. Harvey looked back at Martha who gave him an encouraging nod before he cleared his throat.

"You look like you're in deep thought about something, sport," he commented cautiously, "Is there something on your mind?"

David stopped batting his peas across his plate and lifted his head. His wide, brown eyes stared into Harvey's soul as if searching for something. Harvey forced a comforting smile to encourage him to share but the boy dropped his gaze back down to his plate.

"It's okay David. If there's something bothering you, you can tell us," Martha reassured.

Still, David remained quiet and shrunk lower into his chair. After a few more tense moments, he straightened his back and looked up.

"What am I?" He asked.

The question surprised both adults. Harvey locked eyes with Martha who looked panicked. Then she turned her attention back to their son.

"What do you mean honey? What's this all about?" She asked.

David lowered his head again then extended his arm over the table. They both watched as he dug into his wrist and pulled back a thin layer of rubber skin, revealing a clear plastic casing with hardware inside. Harvey's jaw clenched and he heard Martha let out a quiet gasp. David continued to hold out his arm, waiting for some response, then released rubber to fall back into place.

"I found out I could do that a week ago," he explained, "I thought everyone was like that until I showed Tommy today and he said I was a freak. He said I was just a robot that you guys bought because you couldn't have a real kid. Is that true?"

His eyes went back and forth between his parents, each time becoming waterier. Harvey glanced at Martha. She stared at their son solemnly, wanting to say something but not knowing how to take the pain away. He set his fork down and took in a deep breath.

"David, do you remember our talk about where babies come from?" He asked.

The boy nodded as tears rolled down his cheeks.

"Well, before you... came to be, your mother and I were trying to have a child of our own, but the doctor told us that we wouldn't be able to. So instead, we decided to build a child with technology and that is how you were....born."

With each word, David's face twisted in agony, and he started to whimper. Martha jumped up from her seat and rushed over to hug him.

"Oh David, we still love you even though you are a robot," she assured.

This only made the boy cry louder as he buried his face in her chest. Harvey sighed again and looked at the clock, knowing it was going to be a long night.

Human_Conscious.exe

"This is a terrible idea guys."

Savanna watched as the last two of the friend group play rock-paper-scissors. Adam and Candice already assumed their positions at their desktops while Emil watched the match carefully. Jordan and Tristen pounded their fists in the air three times before flashing a flat hand and a fist.

"Yes!" Jordan screamed, jumping a little off the ground, "I'm going into cyberspace!"

"Damn, oh well. We all set up?" Tristen asked.

"All set over here," Candice reported, "The code looks good, and everything's connected."

"Is anybody listening to me?" Savanna shouted, "Why are we testing this equipment on a human first? We don't know what's going to happen!"

"Aw, come on! Don't be a party pooper!" Jordan retorted, "Worst case scenario is that the thing's not going to work."

"Are you sure about that?"

"Well, we'll just have to find out," Tristen said, "Let's get you hooked up man."

The young computer programmer eagerly hopped onto the couch where a crude helmet connected to several wires sat on the table next to it. He relaxed in his seat while Tristen fitted the helmet and heart monitor on him. Savanna continued to watch them, slack-jawed and wondering if she was dreaming. Her stunned silence was interrupted when Emil patted her on the shoulder.

"You brought the stuff, right?" He asked.

"Yeah, I did. I was hoping you guys would come to your senses by the time I got here," she replied.

"Yo Savanna! I'm ready for the good stuff!" Jordan shouted.

"Please tell me you guys know what's going to happen," Savanna pleaded, ignoring the man on the couch.

"We've calculated that there's an 87% success rate," Emil replied.

"87%? How do you know?"

"Uh, well, we're kinda just guessing on the exact number," Emil admitted, "But we did install a shut-off system if we fail to make a connection."

Savanna was about to grill him more when she felt someone pat her other shoulder. She turned to see Tristen giving her a thumbs up.

"Ready when you are," he said with a grin.

She wanted so badly to argue more but sighed. They were all worked up and there was no way they were going to back out now. She grabbed her medical bag and stormed over to Jordan's side.

"I better not go to federal prison for this," she grumbled as she pulled out a syringe and a vile.

"The camera footage has already been wiped and the records have been altered. You should be good," Adam said over his screen.

The other two slipped into their chairs and started furiously pounding away at their keyboards. Savanna carefully filled the syringe then checked to make sure there weren't any air bubbles. The machine that the helmet was connecting to started to whir next to her, its hardware blinking rapidly.

"The system's running. Ready when you are," Candice announced.

"I'm ready!" Jordan replied.

"You better come out of this okay," Savanna grunted.

"It's gonna be fine," Jordan assured, "Tell you what, if this doesn't work, I'll by you your drinks for a week."

Savanna just sighed.

"I'm administering now," she said loudly.

Slowly, she injected the drug into Jordan's arm. He watched, breathing heavily, then laid his head down.

"Heartrate's normal. I'm still getting brain signals," Emil said.

"Alright, let's turn on the helmet," Tristen ordered.

Some clacking later and the lights on the helmet went off. Savanna put the vile away and wrapped up the syringe to be disposed of later before sitting on the floor next to the couch.

"His brain waves are synchronizing with the system," Candice announced, "We're almost there."

"How's his vitals Emil?" Tristen asked.

"He's still good. I think we're ready."

"It's matching up! We're ready to connect!" Candice exclaimed.

"Okay! Adam, open the portal!"

"Roger."

All four of them furiously typed on their computers for another minute before they suddenly stopped.

"Is something wrong?" Savanna asked.

"No no. We're just waiting," Tristen explained.

"Waiting for what?"

"Waiting to see if it worked," Candice clarified.

A couple more seconds passed before Adam and Candice's computers started beeping.

"It's done! He did it!" Adam cried.

"Alright, I'm turning on the projector!" Tristen said.

The projector in front of them flashed on then went to a black screen with a single cursor blinking at the top.

"Alright, I'm going to send a message to check if he's responsive," Tristen said, "Hands off the keyboards guys."

Everyone did as they were told, and he typed out a short message. The cursor on the screen continued to blink in the same spot. Savanna bit her lip while everyone else held their breath. Suddenly, the cursor started to move.

I'm in dudes!

The entire room roared in applause. Tristen and Emil high-fived each other while Savanna took a few deep breaths.

"We did it! We finally downloaded a human conscious onto a computer system!" Tristen cried.

"We're gonna be world famous!" Candice shouted.

"NASA's going to be breaking down our doors to get us to work for them!" Emil added.

"Is he okay in there?" Savanna asked.

"Hold on, I'll ask him," Tristen said.

He typed out another message and sent it. A few seconds later, the reply appeared.

I'm okay. It's really weird. It's like I'm dreaming in binary.

"This is incredible," Tristen gasped.

While the computer scientist continued to gab among themselves, Savanna continued to watch the screen while her hand reached over to rub Jordan's arm. The cursor continued to blink for a little bit before the next message appeared.

Soooooooo, how do I get out of here?

Down the Sewer Hole

The car engine sputtered for three seconds before going silent. Evan stared at the dashboard, praying to any god who would listen, then turned the key again. More stalling, no starting. This time he counted to five before letting it go. The growing heat in the enclosed car nearly suffocated him. He pounded a fist on the steering wheel out of frustration.

"God fucking damn it!"

He picked up his phone and tapped the screen. The battery icon in the corner showed five percent. Another hit to the steering wheel; this time his palm stung. Swallowing what was left of his pride, he opened his car door to step out into the gas station parking lot. The bright light from the sun nearly blinded him as the hot New Mexico heat fried his skin. He locked his car then ran into the convenience store just a few feet away. Christian talk-show radio greeted him as he walked up to the counter where an old attendant stood. The man looked frail, the years had clearly not been kind to him, but trustworthy.

"My car battery just died. Could you help me jump it?" Evan asked, "I have the cables."

The old man stared at him before shaking his head.

"'fraid I can't," he said in a raspy voice, "Store policy is I can't leave the store while a customer's on the premises. Besides, I don't own a car. My son drives me here on his way to work."

"Well, when does your son get here?"

"He'll probably be here 'round five."

Evan looked up at the digital clock hanging on the wall next to the cigarettes. It wasn't even one o'clock yet. Just as he was about to give up, another idea came to him. He pulled out his wallet and flipped through the numerous punch cards and receipts before finding a worn-out triple A card. It had turned grey from the gunk in the wallet, but it was still legible and in date.

"Can I use your phone real quick? Mine's about to die."

"Sure. Just don't leave the store with it."

The old man took the wireless landline phone next to the register from its cradle and handed it over. Evan shuttered thinking about putting the gross, shiny receiver to his ear but ignored it to dial the number on the back of the card. Once he gave the woman on the other end his information, he got the estimated wait time and sighed. He accepted it and hung up the phone to give back to the attendant.

"Not lookin' good?" The old man asked.

"They said they'll be here in about two hours," Evan replied.

A loud whistle passed through the old man's lips.

"That's bad. Usually they're more on top of these things. My son had a tire blow out just last month and they were with him in about thirty minutes. Well, while you're waitin', you wanna top off your tank?"

"No thanks, I put in half a tank at my last stop, I think I'll be good-" Evan stopped midsentence to rethink. The gears in his head whirled as he tried to remember how long ago the last gas station was. "You know what? A few gallons won't hurt."

"Was 'bout to say, you weren't lookin' too sure there?" The old man remarked with a toothy grin, "How much ya think you need?"

"Oooooooh, maybe ten dollars' worth. The next town isn't too far right?"

"It's about eight miles."

"Maybe twenty then."

As he pulled out his debit car, Evan remembered that he didn't have a gas can. He stepped away from the counter to look at the small canisters on a bottom shelf by all the car products. As he pondered his limited options, he heard a light thunk on the counter. A large, discolored gas can was now in front of him with the old man's hand on top of it.

"I know it's against policy, but the prices of those things are stupid," he spat.

Evan couldn't help but smile in appreciation. After paying for the gas, he went out to the dusty pumps that looked like they would fall apart if he touched them. The nozzle was hot to the touch, but he dealt with it as he stuck the end into the can and squeezed the handle. As poured into it, his mind began to wonder about what he was going to do once he got to the next town.

Just as the nozzle clicked, he heard something metal being dragged on the ground. Confused, he looked around before noticing the lid of the sewer hole in the middle of the road had been pushed to the side. A gloved hand popped out of the opening and a man in a purple suit with matching top hat pulled himself out from underground. Evan's jaw dropped. The man stood up to dust off his clothes before strolling past the pumps to the convenience store as if it were normal.

Evan watched in bewilderment, not sure if what he saw was real. Still dazed, he hung up the nozzle then returned to his car. He contemplated whether it was hot enough to cause hallucinations while filling his tank. Just as he was about to write it off as a daydream, the convenience store door jingled as it opened. He turned his head just in time to see the purple suited man walk back across the parking lot with a plastic bag in his hand. His eyes followed and watched him disappear back down the sewer hole, pulling the metal lid closed behind him.

It took Evan a minute to register what he saw before he shook his head violently to get rid of the cobwebs. Part of him wanted to go right up to the manhole to investigate while another wanted to continue to believe what he saw was an illusion. Picking up the gas container, he made his way back into the store. He returned the container to the front counter then beelined for the water bottles to contemplate his next move. When a vague idea formed, he grabbed a bottle of spring water and hurried back to the register. The old man rang him up while he cleared his throat.

"Did I really just see that back there?"

"See what?" The old man asked.

"The guy. In the purple suit?"

"Oh yeah, that's Ed."

Evan raised an eyebrow.

"……Ed?"

"Yeah, Ed something or other. He told me his full name once, but I forgot it. It's a long one."

"Does he…normally come out of the sewer hole like that?"

"Yeah, that's where he lives."

"Uh, what?"

The water and his debit card were pushed back across the counter but Evan ignored them.

"Yeah, he's an odd one. He usually comes up once a day to get necessities. Sure does scare quite a few folks whenever he pops up."

"But.... why?"

The old man shrugged.

"Not sure. He said something about needing a quiet place to retire but I'm not sure why he chose there specifically. To each their own, I suppose."

Evan's hands finally took the debit card and slipped it back into his wallet. Then he took the water bottle and twisted off the cap. As he sipped his drink, he looked up to the clock that showed it was a little past one. The mental gears spun faster until the words made their way out with the grace of a belch.

"Do you think he likes visitors?"

Regret immediately hit him while the old man shrugged again.

"Don't know. He's never invited me, and I haven't seen anyone else go down there."

Evan wanted so badly to forget the topic and spend the rest of his two hours relaxing in the air-conditioned store and talking to the old man about politics or something. But the pervasive thought remained, itching until he couldn't ignore it.

"I think I'll go ask if I can visit," he said.

Now it was the old man's turn to look surprised. But he nodded understandingly.

"Yeah, I suppose it wouldn't hurt to ask," he agreed.

"If the triple A truck comes out while I'm gone, will you come get me?"

"Sure, so long as you tell me what he's got down there. You'll probably need these."

He ducked down behind the counter then popped back up with a dirty pair of work gloves in hand.

"That lid'll burn ya this time of day."

Evan looked at the gloves, imagining the amount of dirt and germs that clung to them both inside and out. Once he realized he was staring too long, he snapped back to reality to take them.

"Uh, thanks. Wish me luck."

With a nod and a handshake, he was outside crossing the parking lot. Evan tried to tell himself that he could always turn back. Who cared what some wacko did in the sewers? What business did he have there? Before he could come up with more questions, he found himself standing inches from the sewer hole. The brown lid was worn from years of being run over by blissfully unaware drivers; not even the name of the closest city was legible.

After trying and failing to read the words, Evan gave up and pulled on the gloves. The tiny grains of dirt and unsettling stiffness of long-dried sweat brought a shiver up his spine. With his protection on, he pulled the lid up by the small holes drilled into it, feeling the heat through the fabric. He shimmied the heavy saucer to the side then peered down. The drop was pitch black; he could barely see anything beyond a few feet even with the aid of the sunlight. A black iron ladder led downwards but that was it. More questions bounced around in his head when he heard a shuffle from below.

"Who goes there?" A strained voice called out.

The owner of it sounded more normal than Evan expected. He took a second to come up with a reply.

"Hello! I'm the guy who was topping off his tank in the parking lot."

He waited for a response, but the uncomfortable silence prompted him to give more information.

"The old man at the store tells me you live here. Is that true?"

"Of course it's true! Why else would I be down here?"

"Well, I don't know. I've never heard of someone living in a sewer before."

"Well that's your fault for not knowing," the voice retorted, "Now what do you want from me?"

Evan could hear the apprehension in the voice. He licked his lips before proceeding.

"Um, I was wondering if it would be okay if I came down there. You seem like an... interesting guy and I have to hang around here for two hours anyways."

"You want to have afternoon tea with me?" The man asked in surprise.

The idea to go back to the store returned again but he held his ground.

"Um, yeah, sure. I can do tea."

"Oh goodness! I haven't had anyone down here in ages! Come in, come in! But please be sure to close the lid before you come down."

Evan carefully climbed in and, after making sure the ladder was secure, pulled the lid over him with all his strength. Now he was trapped in darkness. Before he started his descent, the voice pipped up again.

"Just a minute! Let me turn on the lights for you."

The inky black abyss suddenly lit up with yellow lights. After a few watery blinks, he was able to see his own two hands clenching onto the ladder for dear life. With his path now illuminated, he started his climb downwards. The tunnel was nothing but bare concrete for the first ten feet until the chipped edges of maroon wallpaper appeared. Soon he came across an antique lamp coming out of the wall with little jeweled tassels dangling from its the orb shade. A few more rungs down he found himself surrounded by all kinds of random antiques from different eras. Some were in perfect condition while others looked like they were rescued from the garbage. When he looked down, he saw that the collection stretched to the rest of the tunnel.

"Hurry down now! I'm getting the kettle ready, and it should be done soon," the man called up. His voice sounded farther away than the last time.

"Take your time! I'm just looking at your.... collection."

"It's marvelous, isn't it? I can tell you all about it when you're down here. Do you take cream and sugar with your tea?"

"Er, no thank you. I'll take mine plain."

"Alrighty then. I'll see if I have anything for us to nibble on."

There were faint footsteps disappearing further into the tunnel then everything was quiet again. At that moment, the sense of worry that had followed Evan up to that point had vanished. As he climbed down, he gazed at the stuff that was either glued or pinned to the wall. There were old toys, glass figurines and knickknacks, China plates, rusted bottlecaps, dented instruments, and many more things. Even the lamps that lit the way were all different shapes and styles.

Enthralled by everything, Evan nearly panicked when his foot hit solid ground instead of a metal bar. He turned around to see a doorway covered by a heavy purple curtain. It had been haphazardly pulled closed, allowing a thin bar of light to peek through. An instant breakout of goosebumps alerted him to the drop in temperature. Suddenly a loud clang came from the other side followed by a hushed curse that echoed strangely. Nervousness returned to his stomach as he pulled the curtain to the side.

The pungent flea market smell hit him as he nearly tripped down a few more steps. Once he collected himself, he looked around at a room that was twice the size of a lecture hall and shaped like a dome. Random antiques were strewn everywhere with slightly more organization than the tunnel. There was a painting area, a statue area, a China set area, and more. There was even a side room full of books with a large velvet armchair and side table in the center. A variety of streetlamps sprouted up around the room, providing dim lighting.

Beyond the forest of old cabinets and garden decorations, Evan saw a kitchen table and stove on the other side of the room. There was the purple suited man bustling about putting plates of something on the table. A copper kettle on the stove whistled as steam rushed out of its spout. The man pulled it off the hotplate to pour the contents into a colorful teapot. When he spotted Evan taking in everything, a wide grin stretched across his face.

"Just in time! Please come over!"

His cheery voice bounced off the walls, ringing in Evan's ears. He made his way across the labyrinth of stuff; the smell of ancient wood and decaying fabric clogged his nose as he went. After tiptoeing around a plastic grass patch covered in little fairy statues, he was finally in the kitchen. Contrary to the extravagance in the rest of the room, the table was plain with several small scratches and black stains on its surface. Eight chairs surrounded it, all of various styles. There was a ready teapot and some plates of food at the head of the table where his host was.

At long last, Evan got a good look at the strange man that lured him down there. Physically, he was unassuming. His skin was a little on the pink side and his brown hair was receding. The suit he wore looked like it was from the late 1800s; it was as if he leaped out of one of the old photographs in the tunnel. He finished the placement of the dinnerware then paused to look up.

"Is something the matter?" He asked.

"Uh....no," Evan replied, taking a seat next to him while removing his gloves.

Fresh steam emanated from the teacup that was placed in front of him. He reached out to grab it, but the hot porcelain made him retract his hand. Meanwhile, the man was already sipping from his cup blissfully.

"It's so nice to have company. No one has visited me in ages," he mused, "You'll have to excuse the dust down here. Had I known someone was coming, I would have tidied up."

"Ah.... I'm sorry for barging in," Evan mumbled.

The man continued to drink his tea while Evan watched him closely. Besides the setting and attire, there was nothing immediately alarming about him. Perhaps a little too cheery and oblivious but he couldn't pick out any obvious signs of mental illness he learned about in his Psych 101 course. He went for his teacup again, but it was still scalding to the touch. He sighed and cleared his throat.

"So, the guy at the station told me your name is Ed," he started awkwardly.

"Did he now? How funny!"

"It's...not Ed?"

"Oh no, my parents would never have settled on such a name. But my full name is a mouthful for most, so I don't begrudge him for forgetting."

"He said that it was really long."

"Yes, yes, it is. I'll need to remind him of my real name when I see him again. But allow me to properly introduce myself."

He finished his first cup then poured himself another.

"My name is Edward William Abiran Herman Othenial Merriwether," he said without a pause or breath before giving his usual smile. "However, if you find it easier, you may call me 'Ed'."

"Er, right," was all Evan could say after a short pause, "How did you end up with that name?"

"It's a funny story, really. You see, I'm the youngest of five children. My four elder siblings were all beautiful, charming girls but my parents always hoped for a son. Then I was born. They figured they'd never have another child, let alone another son, so they decided to give me all the boy names they had thought of for my sisters along with a new one just for me."

"That's.... an interesting story," Evan remarked.

"It makes for a fun conversation starter," Ed admitted, "Now please, tell me your name."

"Oh, right. My name is Evan."

"Evan. Evan. Evan... Short but to the point. How charming! It's nice to meet you Evan. Please help yourself to refreshments."

Evan looked down at the several plates of goodies in front of him. He picked up what he thought was a strawberry Danish and nibbled on it while he glanced around the room to find something to ask about. His eyes went from a mounted moose head to a portrait of a naked lady leaning against a golf bag, to a bust of Athena, then eventually back to Ed drinking his tea.

"So, what's with all the antiques?" He blurted out.

"Hm? Ah yes. I did promise to tell you all about this, didn't I?"

"Yeah. You've got a little bit of everything here. Is there a rhyme or reason to any of it?"

Another chuckle escaped Ed's lips.

"I'm afraid not, no. I started with collecting China and pottery then it expanded to collecting anything I found interesting or amusing. One of these days I'll need to construct another side room like with my library."

"Why go through the trouble of building in a sewer? And how would you even do all that construction down here?"

"Oh, I have my ways. Nothing is impossible," Ed replied with a laugh, "I prefer to have all my possessions in one place so this would be the most logical option."

"You could relocate everything to a mansion or storage facility."

"I suppose but moving is so bothersome and it's much quieter down here."

"Uuuuh..."

Evan tried to work through the mental gymnastics of Ed's plan while he reached for his finally cooled teacup. He thought hard on his next question as he took a sip. When his eyes fell on one of the many stacks of books in the "library", he opened his mouth.

"Sooooo, you read a lot?" He asked.

"When I have the time, yes," Ed replied as he picked up a chocolate chip cookie.

"Did you read all of those books?"

"Goodness no! I'm barely halfway through. I've taken up the bad habit of buying anything that catches my eye then forgetting about it."

"Do you have a favorite book?"

Ed's face scrunched up while he thought.

"Hm, let me see...No, I don't believe I have a particular favorite. There are a few that I return to from time to time, but I wouldn't single out any one of them as my 'favorite'. I like different stories for different reasons. Have you a favorite?"

"Ah, y-yeah. Let me think about it," Evan searched his memory for a title to drop, "I guess I really liked Slaughterhouse Five when we read it in high school."

"Ah! 'So it goes'," Ed chimed, "Excellent choice. And an interesting author as well. But I suppose all authors are interesting characters in their own ways. I remember having tea with Charles Dodgson some time ago when I was traveling in England. Very nice man but horribly shy."

"Charles......Dodgson?"

"Oh, sorry. You probably know him by his pen name. Lewis Carroll?"

".... wait. The Alice and Wonderland guy?"

"Exactly."

"You.... met him?"

"Yes, it was a Sunday in spring if I recall correctly. I believe he had published that book a few months earlier. He probably wouldn't believe that it would become a sensation."

He continued to prattle on while Evan stared at him in disbelief. The idea of his host having a mental disorder came up again. Perhaps schizophrenia or some other delusional disorder.

"But enough about my collection, tell me about yourself."

Evan snapped back to attention.

"Huh? Myself? Why?"

"Well, a young man who pops in for a visit out of nowhere must be an interesting person."

"Uh, actually, I'm a pretty boring guy. Especially compared to you."

"Nonsense! Everyone has something interesting to share. Where are you from?"

A chill went up Evan's spine as the spotlight shifted onto him. Telling a guy he spent the last thirty minutes figuring out was not something he had planned on. But as Ed continued to stare, he felt backed into a corner. He sighed as he reminded himself that he was never going to see the man again.

"Well, I'm from Texas but my family is originally from Pennsylvania. We moved when I was five because of my dad's work."

"Interesting. What does your father do?"

"He's a mechanical engineer. He used to get ping-ponged around a lot, but we finally settled in Texas. I'm actually studying computer science in school-"

"Amazing! I bet you'll have employers knocking down your door."

"Well.... not.... really."

A familiar weight pulled as his gaze fell into his half-empty cup.

"What's the matter?" Ed asked.

"It's nothing," Evan tried to lie. He could feel Ed's disbelieving eyes on him, "Well, it should be nothing. It's just- It's really stupid."

"Try me."

His mind screamed at him to keep his mouth shut. However, the weight inside was becoming unbearable. He needed to get this out; he needed to say something.

"Well, I don't think I want to make a career out of it. My parents pushed me to go into computer science and I tricked myself into thinking that that's what I wanted. I mean, I'm good at it. I'm all about programming and math and so it would make sense that I do this as a career, right?"

His heartbeat started picking up. Looking at his audience, he was surprised to see Ed's focus glued on him. He was actually listening. It felt nice, so he continued.

"I just don't get it. I'm good at something, it makes everyone proud, and I have a future in this industry. But the more and more I think about doing this for the rest of my life, the more I just want to jump ship and disappear. If I say anything to my parents or anyone else in the family, they'll tell me that it's all in my head. But it's not that. I feel so trapped."

He paused again to look up. His host was still listening, wearing the same compassionate expression as before.

"What about your friends? What do they say?" Ed asked.

Evan let out a bitter laugh.

"I only have, like, three friends and all of them are in different schools."

"Oh."

For the first time, Ed's face dropped from its normal cheeriness. Evan nodded in agreement.

"Honestly, there are days where I hope I get hit by a bus or electrocuted or something so that I'll get just enough brain damage for everyone to leave me alone," he admitted, "I'm actually on one of those 'self-reflection road trips' right now to clear my head. The plan was that I'll have everything figured out by the time I get back home. But the more I think about everything, the more uncertain I am. I'm more confused than ever and it fucking blows."

He finally stopped to take a long breath. Now the tea was ice cold but he still downed it in one gulp to wash away his cotton mouth. From the corner of his eye, he saw Ed waiting patiently. Evan couldn't help but laugh again.

"I'm sorry, I'm just complaining here," he muttered, "I wish I made more sense."

"No, no. It's perfectly fine. We all need to get things off our chest every once in a while," Ed assured.

He took the pause in the conversation as a chance to refill their cups. Evan didn't mind the hot tea now, the cup felt nice in his hands.

"Thank you. You have no idea how long I've been holding that in."

"We've all been there at some point," Ed replied, "I was in your shoes many years ago. Essentially, I was given two choices: join the family business and make a small fortune or be tossed out of the house."

"What did you do?"

Ed's eyes gleamed as he grinned.

"I chose to go my own way, and to this day I don't regret it. There have been plenty of mistakes made and bouts of bad luck, but it was all worth the freedom. I've had so many adventures and met so many amazing people along the way. I remember it like it was yesterday. Riding a hot air balloon over Cambodia, going to parties in Morocco, riding a train through the frontier. Even feeling the salty winds of the ocean when I sailed from the tip of Florida to Brazil holds a special place in my heart. Those were the days. I miss them greatly."

Now it was his turn to pause for a drink.

"Well, you can still go out and travel now, right?" Evan asked, "I'm sure lot has changed since your last adventure."

The man smiled then shook his head.

"That is a nice thought, but I'm afraid this world is not meant for the likes of me anymore. My last rendezvous landed me in a spot of trouble with law enforcement," Evan noticed a hue of pink appear in Ed's cheek, "No, this world has no room or patience for an old relic like me. It's best that I stay in retirement."

Despite the happy expression, Ed's shoulders drooped in defeat. Before Evan could say anything, he inhaled sharply.

"Oh well, what's passed is past," he said like a deflating balloon, "I'm just happy I experienced what I could."

Evan sipped his tea, processing everything that had been said. He glanced around the dome of antiques again, stopping at anything that looked cool and wondering about their history.

"So, what's the story behind-"

CLANG! CLANG! CLANG!

The abrupt sound scared the both of them.

"What on Earth was that?" Ed balked.

It took Evan a moment to remember.

"That must be the old guy at the gas station. I asked him to come get me when triple A got here," he explained.

"Ah, then you must be on your way now."

For a split second, Evan thought he saw a flicker of sadness in Ed's face, but it was soon gone. He got up slowly while his host gathered the dishes.

"Would you like to take something with you for your journey? A little snack?" He asked.

"No, no thank you. I think I'm okay."

"Well, wait a moment."

Ed rushed over to the kitchen cabinets and returned with a checkered handkerchief. He piled various goodies in the center of the cloth then tied it all up in a little bundle and handed it over.

"Would you please give these to Gregory before you leave? I've been meaning to do so earlier but I always forget."

"Gregory?"

"The 'old man at the store'. I know it's against that ridiculous store policy for him to eat in front of customers, but I'm worried about him. He's been getting awfully skinny this past year."

Evan stared at the bundle before taking it.

"O-okay. I'll be sure to give this to him."

A smile stretched across Ed's face as he extended an arm.

"It was so nice talking to you Evan. I enjoyed the company," he said while they shook hands, "And don't be a stranger. If you're ever in the area, don't hesitate to drop in for a visit."

"Uh, thank you. It was nice talking to you too," was all Evan could say.

He grabbed his gloves before turning to brave the maze of antiques while he heard clanking glassware behind him. For a brief moment, he wanted to turn around to bid a final goodbye but that felt too cheesy, so he went through the curtains without a word.

Again, the metallic clangs echoed down the tunnel, nearly deafening him. Evan put the knot of the bundle in his mouth and slipped on the gloves before he started the climb. He sped past the myriad of collectables and crossed the edge of the wallpaper. With the last bit of strength he had left, he pushed the lid up a crack. The long end of a monkey wrench slid in, almost smacking him in the face. It helped to lift up the lid and Evan blinked a few times before pulling himself up onto the hot desert road. The lid fell back into place with a loud gong.

"You okay?" He heard the old man asked.

He paused a moment for his vision to adjust, then took the bundle out of his mouth and turned to the old man. Under the sun's rays, he looked a lot tanner than in the store. Evan looked at the nametag pinned to his shirt that simply read 'Greg'.

"Yeah. I'm fine," he replied.

"Well, the guy you've been waiting for is here, so I came ta get ya like I promised."

"Thank you," Evan turned his body to face him then handed over the bundle. "Before I forget, he wanted me to give this to you."

"What is it?" Greg asked, eyeing it with suspicion.

"Snacks."

"Huh. I didn't know he had anything down there other than what he bought from here."

"Yeah, he's a pretty interesting guy."

"Didja get his name?"

"I did. It was Edward, um, uh," Evan's eyes rolled up to think but came to a blank. He laughed, "I can't remember now. He said we can call him Ed though."

"Ha!"

They walked out of the middle of the road to a white truck with a logo parked next to Evan's car where a very confused roadside assistant stood. As they approached, Evan took off the gloves to hand back to Greg.

"Sorry about that! I was having some tea," he explained.

The guy continued to look at him like he had a third eye.

"So...you just need your car jumped?" He asked.

"Yeah."

"Okay. Pop the lid for me and we'll get you going."

Evan opened the driver's door and a wave of heat smacked him in the face. He held his breath as he pulled the lever to pop the hood while the triple A guy came around with cables and spare battery in hand. As he prepped everything, Evan stepped away to allow his car to air out.

"Wow! These are just like the ones my wife used to make!"

He looked over to see Greg munching on a cookie while he carefully cradled the opened bundle in his palm.

"Really?"

Greg nodded and swallowed.

"Yes. She was the queen of baking back in the day. Won first prize in the pie contest a few times," his face glowed with pride but swiftly changed to grief, "She died earlier this year."

"Oh! I'm so sorry," Evan gasped.

"It's alright. She was havin' a hard time towards the end. Cancer. Been struggling with it for the last two years. Now she's at peace. 'least she's not hurtin' anymore."

For a moment, Evan wanted to put a hand on his shoulder to comfort him.

"Alright, try and start it."

The guy waited by the car hood with the cables all hooked up. Evan nodded quickly then hopped into the driver's seat to turn the key. The engine revved up in seconds, roaring with energy.

"Looks like it's your lucky day," the guy shouted as he removed the cables, "Drive it around for about fifteen minutes before shutting it off. I recommend getting the battery replaced as soon as possible."

"Thank you!" Evan shouted back.

The guy gathered up his cables and closed the hood while Evan rolled down the windows. The AC soon brought the temperature down to a comfortable level. As the triple A truck pulled away, he spotted Greg moseying his way back to the front of the convenience store.

"Hey!"

Greg turned to face him.

"Ed said he doesn't get much company and he seemed pretty lonely down there. I'm sure he won't mind another visitor. Why don't you go down and see him sometime?"

A perplexed expression replaced Greg's somber mood. He bobbed his head back and forth, arguing with himself, then he looked Evan right in the eye.

"I'll consider it. I have some time after work I think," he said with a grin.

Evan shot him a thumbs up.

"Thank you for the help today!"

"No problem son! You take care now!"

Then he disappeared back into the store. Evan pulled out of the parking spot and drove to the exit. He stopped just before turning to look at the ground. The sewer lid lay still as if nothing had happened. He chuckled as he pulled out onto the road and sped off.

The Dancing Cat

Matt stared at the sheet of paper that had been placed on his desk ten minutes ago. All around him the other students shoved their homework and notebooks into their backpacks, but he just sat there. He tried to focus on his own handwriting, retracing the mathematics he had written two days ago, but the red marks kept grabbing his attention. Finally, his eyes returned to the score on the top of the page that made his stomach sink.

2/10: Please see me after class.

He blinked but the score was still there. The bell rang and everyone darted out the door, escaping into the weekend ahead of them. Once most of the class was gone, he finally took the paper and tucked it into his backpack. He slung it over his shoulder and pulled the hood of his grey hoodie over his head. He almost made it out the door when his hood was suddenly pulled off from behind. He spun around to see his algebra teacher Mr. Mason.

"Matt, can I have a word with you?" He asked.

They both knew there was only one option. Matt nodded submissively and followed him to the front desk. Mr. Mason sat in his office chair and turned it to look at the tween in front of him.

"I'm going to be honest with you Matt, I have no idea what to do with you," he began bluntly, "This is the third quiz you failed. The test is in two weeks, and you have shown no sign of understanding the concepts I've been discussing in class. Your homework looks good, but you haven't been able to apply what you've learned to the quizzes which raises a lot of questions on my end. Can you please explain to me what's going on? Is there anything I can do to help you pass this class? Talk to me."

Matt refused to look the man in the eye. His stomach was so twisted up in a knot that he could only look down at his shoes. A few moments passed before he gave a half-hearted shrug. Mr. Mason let out a sigh.

"I didn't want to do this Matt, but I emailed your parents about this. You started the year off fine, but you've plateaued these last few months. At this point you have two options: come to school early for tutoring or drop back down to pre-algebra. The choice is yours. Have a good weekend."

The only thing Matt could do was nod to the floor before spinning around to leave. The hallway was still crowded by the time he made it to his locker. He spun in the combination and opened it to retrieve his English textbook for the weekend homework, ignoring the "secret admirer" letter that fell to the floor. Suddenly, his locker door slammed on his head, briefly smashing his throat against the metal frame. He pulled himself out just in time to see a group of guys laughing as they walked away while Jeff, their leader, sneered at him. Matt glared at their backs as he closed the door and did one last spin of the dial to jumble the combination.

Soon, he was back in the current of middle schoolers that went down to the first floor and out to the waiting line of buses parked along the pickup zone. Matt shuffled towards his bus but stopped when he spotted Jeff and a couple of his lackies in the windows, all wearing a shit-eating grin. His molars bit the inside of his cheek. A wave of anger undid the knot in his stomach, and he straightened up his posture. He raised his middle finger in the air, not caring who saw it, and strode off in the direction of the main road.

When he reached the first traffic light, he heard the cavalry of buses creak their way out of the school parking lot. He somewhat regretted his decision, but it was too late now. The light changed and Matt sped across the intersection. Once he was on the other side, he pulled the other backpack strap over his free shoulder to distribute the weight compressing his spine. He reached into his pocket for his phone but felt nothing. A brief panic stopped him before remembering that he wouldn't get it back until after dinner. Or that's what he thought an hour ago. He groaned then resumed his slow pace.

One of the school buses passed him and he heard a taunting voice scream "faggot!" He didn't need to look up to see who it was; better to pretend not to hear it. With each step he took, his mind played back the day's events until the daydreaming began. Visions of knocking on Jeff's door then beating him to a pulp while his little sister watched. Or figuring out where Mr. Mason lived to slash his tires or plant a pipe bomb under his porch. Or sneaking out at night to set fire to the trees outside of school and watching the whole place burn to the ground. These fantasies brought a smile to his face.

A loud car horn blared into Matt's ear, pulling him back to reality. He looked up to the sign showing the little walking man giving him the right of way then flipped the driver off while he crossed the street. The driver sped away behind him, revving his engine. Matt growled but stopped when he recognized a familiar turn-in. It was a large lawn with a black tar road leading to a children's playground. A couple of kids ran around the woodchip gravel while a parent watched them. He froze in his spot, hypnotized by the happy nostalgia of when he used to be there, not a care in the world. Then he shook himself back to reality and continued on his way.

The next crosswalk was the busiest intersection of the entire route. Matt groaned, knowing that even if he hit the button to cross, it was going to take a while. Regardless, he pressed the giant chrome bulb and leaned on the pole to wait. Now more than ever, he wanted his phone to at least go on Snapchat or play some music. Something to keep him from thinking about every awful thing that happened that day. To his right he saw an elderly man waiting on a bench next a bus stop to get to the city and the hub that can take anyone anywhere, no questions asked. Matt slid his hand into his other pocket to feel his wallet. There was a twenty-dollar bill folded up in the old, faux leather. All that stood in his way was the ten or so steps.

Just as he was about to move, something from the garden park on the other side of the street caught his eye. It looked like the tips of rabbit ears peeking out from the bushes. But instead of hopping around like an animal would, they were swaying and bobbing to a slow tempo. Matt watched as the little ears made their way to break in the shrubbery where people could enter the green oasis.

What sashayed out into the open was a cat standing up on its hind legs. Its fur was light gray, almost white, and had what looked like a red Christmas scrunchie around its neck with little bells sewn onto it. As it tip-toed onto the sidewalk, it did a little twirl with the most content smile on its fuzzy lips. Matt's eyes widened in disbelief. He looked over to the elderly man to see if he saw it too, but he was busy reading a book. When he looked back, the cat was still twirling and dancing as if it were normal.

Then it pranced over to the crosswalk opposite him. By now, the traffic had lightened up with only a few cars passing by, though the red hand still warned pedestrians to sit tight. The cat paid no mind as it stepped onto the road. In his peripherals, Matt spotted a bright red pickup truck zooming towards the intersection to make the light before it changed. His stomach tightened as he looked to see the cat had made it about half-way across the street, unaware of what was coming. The truck did not look like it was stopping any time soon.

Before he knew what he was doing, Matt darted forward with his arms out. He felt the soft thump of the cat colliding with him, and he scooped it up mid-sprint while loud screeching tires followed him. In seconds, he was on the other side of the road with the cat in his arms and an irate truck driver shouting at him. He looked around in a daze. The crosswalk had finally changed but the cars stayed where they were; their drivers staring at him in amazement. He turned away from them and rushed over to a bench in the park to catch his breath.

After sitting for a few minutes, he felt the cat squirm in his chest. He loosened his grip, and it leapt out of his arms onto the walking path to sit and stare at him with its bright blue eyes. He tried to read its face to gage what it was thinking, but it did nothing else. The cat eventually broke eye contact to lick its paw. As it cleaned its face, the buzzing numbness in Matt's system finally wore off.

"What the hell dude?! Did you not see that truck? You could have gotten killed!" He shouted.

The cat snapped back to attention, looking confused. This only made Matt angrier. Before he continued to berate the feline, he heard a panicked whisper off to the side. He looked up to see two girls from his school staring at him. One of them was visibly anxious while the other scanned him with icy eyes. Matt blinked, realizing he was screaming his lungs out in the middle of a public place to a cat. He closed his eyes and took a deep breath. When he opened them, the cat had relaxed its position but still stared at him. Or at least he thought it did. The more he watched, the more it appeared to be looking through him or just past him. He shook away the thought and grabbed onto his backpack straps.

"Just fucking pay attention next time, okay?" He spat.

He turned around and walked out of the garden park. Traffic had returned to normal but with new cars and faces. He noticed the old man was no longer at the bus stop; he missed his chance. The gears in his head whirred as he tried to formulate another plan of escape. Just as he was calculating the logistics of using his bike to run away, he got the feeling that someone was watching him. When he turned around to find the culprit, a fluffy tail caught his attention. Following him closely was the cat, looking at him with its big eyes. Again, it seemed to be studying the area around him instead of him directly. Matt stopped and the cat paused mid-step.

"Why are you following me? Go home you stupid cat!" He grunted before he continued on his way.

After passing the local pizza shop in the strip mall close to his house, Matt felt the need to look over his shoulder again. The cat was still behind him, still staring with the same fascination as before. He growled then turned around.

"Piss off! I'm not your owner! Why don't you go annoy someone else?"

The cat tilted its head in feigned confusion. Matt stomped forward with one foot, and it scurried to some nearby bushes. Satisfied, he cut behind the strip mall through the backyards of his neighborhood. But as soon as he made it to the pure white sidewalk, he heard a small rustle behind him. Out of the shrubbery, the cat sprung after him, more determined than ever. Now he was scared. He sprinted down the winding path back to his home, his hood flew off and he could hear the jingling of the cat's collar. His lungs burned as they tried to keep up with the sudden activity and a small cramp began to above his stomach.

Finally, he saw the dull blue paneling of his house and used his last bit of energy to bolt up the driveway. At that point his body gave up and he crouched over the steps to the front porch. A few coughs cleared his throat, but his heart still pounded in his chest. Then a tiny jingling reached his ears, and he glanced over his shoulder reluctantly. The cat trotted right up to him and plopped its fluffy butt on the narrow walkway, flicking its tail back and forth. Matt wanted to be mad but the running left him drained. All he could do was twist his body around to sit on the steps and stare back at it.

"Look, I don't know what you're thinking, but please leave me alone. I only saved you back there because...well because you weren't paying attention. I'm not going to take you in! I'm not your owner now! Got that?"

The cat blinked then turned its attention to whatever it had laser-focused on before.

"Are you even listening to me? Leave me alone!"

For several seconds, the cat continued to scan him. The longer it stared, the more insecure he felt. Suddenly, it crouched down and wiggled its body while its gaze stayed fixed on the air by his head.

"W-what are you doing?" Matt stuttered.

In an instant the cat pounced. He barely had time to react before it glided effortlessly over his shoulder. The light woosh of its fur next to his ear caused him to freeze in place until he heard the jingling bells of it landing behind him. Once the shock subsided, he turned around to see the cat on his porch crouched over something. He squinted to see a few skinny, bright red limbs of an unknown creature flailing desperately to escape. The cat, however, had no intention of letting it go. It pinned its prey to the ground then chomped on its neck.

The creature immediately went limp but the cat continued to gnaw at the corpse until it was satisfied with its work. It then turned to a stunned Matt. As if it read his mind, the cat dragged its prey around for him to see. At first, he couldn't figure out what the creature was. He traced the corpse until he noticed the thin tail with an arrow-shaped tip. Its feet were tiny cloven hooves while the arms were human-like. When he looked at the head, he saw the pointy ears and the small horns sprouting from the front of its skull.

Matt looked up to the cat who stepped forward to rub its face onto his nose, purring loudly. Then it took the creature into its mouth and hopped off the porch towards the street, its little bells jingling all the way. He watched it disappear around the round corner of his street then stood up, letting his backpack slide off his shoulders. Then he unzipped the front pocket to retrieve his housekeys, feeling strangely lighter in spirit.

The Romantic

Valentine's Day, of all days. Any other night, Maddie would have gone to the bar for a couple of cocktails to forget her disappointment. But tonight, there was only the loud slam of her front door and violent sobbing as she collapsed to the floor of her one-bedroom apartment. Being ghosted wasn't anything new to her, but it hurt so much worse now. Two and a half amazing dates and the promise of a romantic night on the town were all flushed away by hours of awkwardly waiting in the middle of a steakhouse with the waitstaff refilling her water every twenty minutes. The only thing to come out of it was a piece of cake on the house to ease the pain after she worked her way through a bottle of merlot.

The mad dash out of there was a blur to her but she knew she couldn't even touch the cake after paying her tab. She tried to tell herself it was a gesture of kindness but that didn't prevent her humiliation. With tears still liquifying her mascara, she pulled her coat off and leaned back on the door. That's when she noticed that one of her heels had broken off at some point in her journey home. Her foot began to throb, prompting her to remove the shoe and rub her ankle.

A moment of silence was held for her ruined plans; dreams of laughter, romance, and possible sex all crushed under a metric ton of rejection. Then came the question of what to do now. Patricia and Haley were both out with their boyfriends and Veronica was in the middle of her single ladies' party thrown at the local winery, which, out of pride, Maddie quickly dismissed. So, she sat there, thinking about how she looked like a pathetic little girl who got dumped at the high school dance and how she could fix it.

The answer came when her stomach growled, reminding her that she missed dinner. After removing the other heel, she pulled herself up and hobbled over to the kitchen, heading directly for the refrigerator. Upon opening it, she remembered that she bought mostly fruits and vegetables so she wouldn't go off her diet. The only unhealthy thing in her apartment was the half-pint of Cherry Garcia in her freezer which she tucked away for her 'emergency days'. That wasn't going to be enough for tonight and ordering a whole pizza for herself seemed depressing. She needed to do something to get her mind off of everything. An idea came and she went to the cupboard to pull out a large pot.

Within minutes, she had opened a bottle of wine and was chopping up carrots and celery at a dangerous pace, before pouring them into the pot. She went through each step of her mother's pasta fagioli recipe with the efficiency of an assembly line. During the last, long simmer she sipped on her pinot noir while preparing several slices of buttered toast. Tonight, food was going to make everything better.

Just as she finished the last drop in her glass, she heard a knock on her door. She paused, wondering if she was hearing things, when the knocking came a second time. Then it hit her: it had to be him. The selfish, loathsome bastard crawled his way up to her door with a sob story of being late and a condom in his pocket. That ball of slime had come to weasel his way into her sheets after what he pulled on her.

She squeezed the bulb of the wine glass to the brink of shattering it. There was absolutely no way on Earth or in Hell that she was going to let that snake in after that. She looked over at her kitchen counter for something to confront him with. A wooden spoon? Too mild. A frying pan? Too stereotypical. A chef's knife? Too extreme. Or was it? An evil smile curled on her lips as she grabbed the knife and stormed towards the door, imagining the face he was going to make when he saw her. She waited a moment for dramatic effect then turned the knob and pulled the door open with all her might.

What waited for her on the other side was the stump of a neck with a severed spinal cord poking out from a white puffed collar. No face, no head. Just maroon, exposed flesh. Maddie stared at it in shocked silence while the knife slipped out of her fingers and clanged to the ground. The figure in front of her was dressed in a fine suit with a golden chain ran from its vest to the inside of its coat while its white gloved hands held a top hat and a rose. She blinked once then twice, her mind completely blank.

"...Hello?" Was the only thing she managed to say.

As soon as she spoke, the figure bowed and handed her the rose before letting itself in. She was too baffled to stop it and ended up pushing the door closed. The headless man hung its hat on one of the hooks next to the door then paused before picking up her coat on the floor to hang up next to it. Then it faced her as if waiting for a response. She couldn't begin to imagine what it was thinking. Suddenly, it pulled a handkerchief from its coat pocket and held it out to her. She hesitated before taking it.

"T-thank you," she muttered, "A-actually I'm going to use the restroom for a minute. Do you mind?"

The headless man gave a slight bow which she took as an approval. She hurried into the restroom, shutting the door behind her, and stared directly into the mirror. A million questions swirled in her mind of what she should do next. The handkerchief she was given looked very normal with a colorful floral pattern expertly embroidered along its edges. It definitely felt real. Then she held up the rose. The petals were deep red with a healthy green stem that was freshly cut, just like any other rose in the world.

"This is insane. There's no way this is real," she whispered to herself.

The sound of footsteps slowly moved around her living room, reminding her of her company. She used a wet wipe to clean up her mascara and teased her hair so that it didn't look like she had a mental breakdown only forty minutes ago. Taking one last deep breath, she exited the restroom with the small hope that everything would go back to normal. To her dismay, the headless man was still there, standing in front of a painting of three cartoony women on the beach holding coconut drinks. Maddie walked over to its side.

"It was a gift from a friend," she explained. The headless man turned to her, its stump still disgusting her. "We used to go to New Jersey every summer for vacation. Veronica, the artist, painted this of us while we were at the beach."

She waited for a response or a gesture but none came. Hoping to ease the tension she held out the handkerchief.

"I-I had some wipes in the bathroom and I didn't want to ruin this for you. But thanks for offering."

It took the handkerchief and tucked it back into its pocket. More silence followed as Maddie struggled to figure out what to do. Before she could stop herself, she opened her mouth again.

"I was going to sit down for some soup. Would you like some?"

An immediately feeling of regret came over her. The headless man stretched out an arm, inviting her to lead the way. Every neuron in her brain screamed at her for being stupid as she seated the man in the chair across from hers. By the time she made it to the pot, it was still simmering nicely. She pulled out a pair of bowls and plates from the cupboard and served her "guest" some soup with a few pieces of toast. When she sat down with her own serving, her appetite was long gone. Her fingers fiddled with the end of the spoon, but the sight of the headless man's gruesome stump kept her from eating.

Across from her, it picked up its spoon and started stirring. That's when she realized the idiocy of offering someone with no mouth a bowl of soup, or any food for that matter. For ten minutes they sat in silence, awkwardly playing with the food in front of them. In her mind, Maddie imagined it babbling on and on about its job or the stock market or something. She seriously thought about pouring herself another glass of wine. Suddenly, the headless man straightened its posture, spooking her into saying something.

"Um, so, are you from around here?"

The headless man remained still. She couldn't quite tell what it was doing but she felt stupid for starting off with such a dumb question. Despite this, she continued.

"I'm from Virginia myself. I moved here for school and decided to stay once I got a job." She chuckled a little to herself. "My dad keeps teasing me about how I spent all those years in school just to get a clerk position. It annoying but I can see how stupid that was. Especially with all the debt I have."

Glancing up, she noticed that it had stopped stirring the soup. How something without ears could listen was beyond her. But sitting in silence felt weird so, she proceeded.

"My grandfather lived in the area for a while until my mom made him go live with her. He's been suffering from tremors for a few years now. I used to visit him when I was in school, and we would watch *I Love Lucy* reruns."

Warm memories began to flood her mind, making her smile as she teared up.

"I miss him. It was so nice having family around." She picked up her toast and tore off a piece. "I was supposed to be going out with someone tonight, but that didn't work out. Everyone's busy with their own lives so now I'm all alone. Isn't that pathetic?"

She popped the piece in her mouth and chewed. Her chest felt hollow yet was weighed down with sorrow. Now she really wished she had poured herself another glass of wine. Again, she looked up to the headless man. Its hands were folded together, fingers interlocking. Maddie laughed.

"Honestly, I'm not hungry anymore," she admitted, "I'm sorry."

The room fell silent. She could hear some of the people outside either finally coming home from a romantic night out or driving to the next bar before closing. Then she heard a light tapping on the table. She looked up to see the headless man holding out a hand to her. Instinct told her to read the face but with none there she could only speculate. When it reached closer to her, she cautiously put her hand in its palm. The headless man stood up, gently pulling her from her seat, and led her back into the living room.

So many questions bounced around in her head trying to figure out what was going to happen next. The headless man led her to the center of the room then faced the old stereo in the corner of the room. The machine blipped to life with red lights on its control board instead of the standard blue and started to play a violin solo. Before she could comprehend what had just happened, it put one hand on her hip and lifted her right hand up.

They swayed slowly at first, starting with the familiar waltz until the tempo picked up. The headless man moved quickly while Maddie did her best to keep up, allowing it to guide her through the steps. It shuffled around the room, pulling her along with the occasional spin, until the tempo slowed down again. She took the chance to rest her head on its shoulder to catch her breath. Then, at the peak of the moment, the music abruptly ended, and they stopped. Maddie lifted her head to see the stump again. Along her waist, she felt it's arm still comfortably set on her hip. Without warning, she started to laugh, going from a giggle to shaking hysterics in seconds. She buried her face into the its chest while it supported her. Euphoria washed over her until she was able to stand on her own.

"I'm sorry! I'm so sorry! I'm not laughing at you it's just-" She paused to catch her breath then backed away. "It's just that, this is all so surreal and...I don't really know what to do. This was not how I imagined my night would be like and-...it's been so long since I've danced with someone like that."

She took the time to pause and wipe the tears from her eyes.

"I'm sorry. You must think I'm completely crazy now."

The stereo shut down as the room went silent again. Maddie straightened herself out before facing the headless man with a smile.

"Thank you," she said, "I really needed that."

There was a pause before the headless man took her hand and held it up to where its face would have been. The absurdity of the sight almost made her giggle again until it leaned closer to her face. A soft, warm sensation buzzed on her lips, making her heart skip a beat. When the headless man stepped back, she could feel her cheeks flushing. Just as she was about to say something, it pulled a watch from its pocket and opened it then headed towards the front door.

    Maddie watched, confused by the sudden change in mood as the headless man retrieved its top hat from the hook on the wall and turned to bow one last time. Then it opened the door and disappeared into the hall. She stood still, processing what just happened, before going over to the doorframe to find nothing. The hall was completely empty. Her gaze fell to the floor where she spotted the broken off heel of her shoe laying on the welcome mat.

Searching for Peace

It's twilight now. The suffocating heat of the summer day has finally died down while the refreshing night air begins to settle in. Any children who were playing in the park had long since been dragged home by their parents to enjoy an ice cream and the latest episode of their favorite cartoon. Only a few teenagers remain, taking refuge under the brightly colored jungle gym passing a blunt around. The first few yellow lights of the fireflies begin to flicker in and out to the cadence of the grasshoppers. Above it all the deep blue ocean of the night sky lightly dusted in stars pushed away the vibrant sunset. It won't be long before the moon shows its half-veiled face and even the teenagers will have to leave lest their parents begin to wonder where they were.

All of this I observe from a wooden bench with half a cigarette burning between my fingers, the first one I've had in five years, and a small bag of my belongings by my feet. No one will care about the pollution I am putting in the air. They'd probably just be grateful that I don't set one of the trashcans on fire. I take one more puff of my cigarette before putting it out on the sidewalk. It's almost time. I grab the straps of my bag and stand, taking one final look at the warm security of the park, then turn towards a wall separating the playground from the forest that surrounded it.

Scrawny branches and vines wove into a protective fence while the bushes and trees behind it guarded the secrets that nature wishes to hide from curious eyes. I'm sure there are many rumors of what lies within. Some speculate there is someone living in the forest protecting "their" property with traps and a sawed-off shotgun. Or that it's haunted by specters from a long-forgotten massacre or home to a terrifying creature. A select few heard a very different story; a story only told to those who really needed to hear it.

Everything began about six months ago. I had a job at a software company with a decent income, a promotion on the way, and a fiancée, Maria. I was content; everything seemed to fall into place with only the occasional bump in the road that was quickly resolved. Then one day, out of nowhere, a peculiar feeling began to form in my chest. It was small, but it picked at me in a way that worried me. At first, I ignored it, writing it off as butterflies in my stomach due to the wedding and promotion. However, that feeling began to grow from the size of a needle's prick to a gaping hole as large as a softball.

Its venomous jabs began to taint everything enjoyable in my life. My favorite podcasts turned into meaningless gibberish, my visits to the bar with friends became a chore. The work that I had diligently performed for the last three years became unimportant to me as my world turned into a grey wasteland. My friends took notice and tried to cheer me up with more outings and drinks. I tried to play along, drinking nights away while slurring along to pop songs that everyone else was singing to, but the effects were only temporary. By morning I would wake with a hangover that felt like a jackhammer had been taken to my skull and an increasingly concerned look from Maria.

Weeks went by as my work slowly declined in quality. Out of pity or annoyance, I was told by my supervisor to take a leave of absence to get myself situated. The nagging, hallow feeling grew throughout my entire chest as I would spend days lying in bed with a bottle of liquor nearby. I read books and blogs on getting out of this despair, but nothing seemed to help. Tips given to me by a friend or relative only made it worse. Eventually, they started pulling away. One night, when I finally reached my breaking point, I fell into Maria's arms, babbling about this unexplainable misery, even offering to set her free to find a more suitable man. I cried and cried while she stroked my hair with her long, soft fingers. When I finally finished, I rolled over to my side of the bed.

"I don't know what to do," I told her, "I would do anything to get rid of this horrible thing that's made me so miserable. Anything would be worth trying, at this point."

Maria sat beside me, comforting me, then got out of bed and went to the vanity where she did her makeup every morning. Pushing aside her brushes, she pulled out a small, wooden jewelry box that was cracking in some areas and the little pictures on the side eroded. I vaguely remembered her telling me it was an heirloom from her great grandmother. She removed every glittering piece of jewelry from it and pulled out a yellow slip of paper that looked as if it had been torn from a diary. Returning to my side, she placed the paper in my palm and staring directly into my eyes.

"There's an old man who lives in the historical district right next to the bakery and the chapel. He is blind but if you tell his daughter that you are seeking guidance, she will let you in. He has helped many people who felt lost and needed to be shown a way back to happiness. Do you remember my brother? Years ago, he was struggling with the same misery you're experiencing and when he went to this man for help, he was able to find peace. I still don't know how I feel about miracles, but I know that this man can help you."

Back then, I didn't believe in miracles, but I still grasped the paper tightly and kissed Maria like we had been separated for years. The next morning, I followed the address written on the paper to a small yellow house next to a building with a faded-out bakery sign and a church with a finely manicured lawn. A middle-aged woman stood at the front door, and I told her that I needed guidance from the old man who lived there. She welcomed me inside and led me to a room at the back of the house.

Immediately I was hit with the distinct pungency of incense while the woman left to get drinks. Sitting in the corner of the small room was an elderly man calmly smoking a plain wooden pipe. He was very thin and sickly looking with a short white beard but exuded an aura of contentment. As soon as he heard me enter, he gestured to an aluminum chair close to him which I took. The woman came back with two mugs of coffee then left us to be alone. We sat in silence for a few moments, for I didn't know what to say, until the man cleared his throat.

"I understand you have come to see me. What is it that's troubling you, my boy?"

His voice was so warm and understanding that it startled me. When my initial shock subsided, I took a big sip of the watery coffee before responding.

"Sir, I'm miserable and I don't know why. For months there's been this hollow feeling inside my chest and it's only been growing. I've tried to ignore it with my work and alcohol, but it still clings to me. Now I can't work, and my friends are abandoning me. If this loathsome feeling stays, I might lose everything I hold dear. My fiancée told me that you helped her brother and I'm hoping you can help me. Please tell me how I can get rid of this misery and feel like my old self again."

The old man listened to me patiently and nodded when I finished. He took a sip from his coffee, simmering over what I just told him, then looked at me with his cloudy eyes.

"This misery of yours, have you felt it before?"

"Only a few times when I was younger. But it only lasted a few days at most. It's never gone on this long before."

"I see. Have you done anything to remedy it in the past?"

"Well, whenever I got that feeling, I would do something to occupy my time or surround myself with people, and that would usually work. I've tried that with this episode, but it doesn't work now. What's worse is that I have more to lose now than I did in the past. If I can find a way to get rid of it, everything can go back to normal-"

The old man raised a hand, signaling me to stop. He took a few more sips of his coffee with his eyes closed, then spoke.

"There seems to be something buried deep within you that is causing more distress than the average man. Your previous brushes with this "misery", as you call it, was your soul crying out that something was wrong. You should have listened to it then. From what I can see, the root of your misery and its repair requires more than what I can do for you now in this room. However, I may know something that will help you."

Setting the cup on the ground, he slowly, almost painfully, stood up from the chair and shuffled over to a dresser in the corner of the room. He pulled out the middle drawer and shuffled through its contents, throwing random shirts onto the ground, before retrieving a folded-up piece of paper.

"Long ago my father was suffering from the same ailment. He was a banker, around your age now that I think about it, and already had me with my mother. When his misery became too much for him to bear, he was told to go to the location on this map just as the sun set over the horizon and follow the wooden path to a temple in the woods. There he stayed for seven days and nights by himself. When he returned, he was a happier man and was able to live the rest of his life peacefully."

The old man placed the map in my hands with a smile.

"This is a sacred and secret location. When you come back, I ask that you return this map and never tell a soul where it is. If you truly wish to find inner peace, you must go there alone with an open heart. And please, pack accordingly."

When I got home that night, I booked my flight and packed some necessities. As requested, I didn't go into detail with Maria; only saying that this was the cure to my misery. She understood and even kissed me when she dropped me off at the airport.

Now I am here, with the sun finally setting beyond the trees. I stare into the black void of the forest with my conscience torn in two; my mind telling me this is a waste of time but my gut telling me that I must press forward. Setting my fears aside, I begin to walk along the edge of the forest, flashlight in hand, in search of the wooden path the old man told me about. For several minutes, I find nothing. From the corner of my eye, I notice the fireflies floating in a strange formation. Out of curiosity, I turn off my light and follow them. They guide me through the dark until I hear the sound of my feet hit wood. Relieved, I turn back on my light and continue my way.

The dark mystery of the night swallows me as I slowly walk down the path. Beyond the trees, I hear the faint sound of an owl successfully catching its prey while a possum strolls through the bushes. I admit that I am not comfortable in nature's domain as I'm from the city but still, I march on. After some time, I see a line of lanterns ahead that run along the path, giving some light in this unfamiliar world.

For what seems like hours, I continue walking like a wind-up soldier. The wooden path goes on for eternity as it winds past enormous oak trees and bridged over small streams. I notice the gradual muting of the forest sounds the deeper I travel into the woods. The chirping of crickets and the occasional hooting of an owl faded to silence. The surrealness of the atmosphere has me questioning my reality and mission. However, before my increasing doubts convince me to turn back, I see a strange golden glow appear from between the trees. At first, I assume it's a hallucination or the rest of the lanterns, but this haunting light was too unique for either possibility. It starts as a subtle aura from the distance, jailed behind the crooked tree branches, but slowly grows as bright as the lanterns.

After some time, I can distinguish different colors mixed within it, like a faint patchwork rainbow. Then I realize that it was not one whole mass but several colorful organisms. Suddenly, from the corner of my eye, one of those lights passes me and I am taken aback by what I see. Gently floating close to the ground was a small blue and gold clown fish, swimming through the air as comfortably as it would in water. It swims towards a bush to inspect the leaves then disappears through the trees.

Soon, the night sky is decorated by thousands of colorful aquatic animals from all over the world. A school of rainbow fusiliers made its way through the trees before being thrown into a frenzy by a deep purple barracuda. Along the wooden path, a yellow tiger shark minds its own business while some pink pilot fish swam close to its side. A green and orange striped octopus crawls its way onto the path, forcing me to one side to let it through. From underneath the bushes, I watch as little neon crabs scurry along the forest floor. Just when I think this sight couldn't get any stranger, a massive red humpback whale sails over me, knocking me onto my back in amazement.

For some time, I remain in the spot where I fell, questioning my sanity. A small collection of guppies swirl around my head as if to grab my attention then swim up the path. My legs feel nonexistent, but I gather enough courage to stand and follow them. It's not long before the path ends at the face of a cliff with a wooden ladder hanging down from it. Normally I would turn away due to my fear of heights, but the guppies keep floating above me, beckoning me to join them. I take a deep breath and set my foot on the first rung of the ladder. For a terrify half an hour I climb, not daring to glance down, focusing all my attention on the guppies as they swim in front of me. With every rung tackled, I become more confident with myself, though my arms and legs are becoming weak from exhaustion.

Fortunately for my weary muscles, it isn't long after a short break in my ascent, that I can see the edge of the cliff. With my remaining strength, I quicken my pace to reach the top. Once I clear the last rung, I collapse on the soft grass, praising the ground as if I had reached Paradise. Nothing else matters until the guppies once again swim into my field of vision, reminding me of my goal. As I stand up, I see a dirt path leading to a bright opening in the trees. The light is strong but warm, enticing me to come closer. I sprint towards it, knowing that I have finally reached my destination. Then there's nothing but white light. Its intensity forces me to close my eyes. When I reopen them, I am somewhere else.

I am now on a dock overlooking a lake. The deep purple sky above me is peppered in stars while lanterns hover over the water. The colorful aquatic animals are now floating along the edge of the lake as if they don't dare come closer to the water. I spot a small island sitting in the middle of the lake where a temple stands. Large steppingstones come up from the water, creating a path to it from the dock. There is my destination. With great care, I hop from stone to stone, holding the straps to my backpack tight.

When I reach the island's shore, I remove my shoes out of respect before climbing up the steps of the temple. The wooden structure is painted red, the floors are glossy stone tiles with a long carpet that went straight to the back. At the end of the carpet is an alter where a massive stone clam sat. I walk right up to the clam, not knowing what to expect. As soon as I reach the alter, the stone clam creaks open. I watch as it reveals a perfectly spherical pearl the size of a basketball resting on an indigo pillow. The pure white shine of its surface is otherworldly; I want to run my hands on it but don't. Suddenly, a soft but clear voice breaks the quiet moment.

"Come closer."

The words come so abruptly that I freeze.

"Who was that?" I ask, trembling.

"It was I."

My attention focuses back on the pearl. I glance around the alter but there are no sound speakers nor anyone else in the temple. The voice comes again.

"Please come closer so that I may see you more closely."

Uneasiness still grips me as I climb into the clam's mouth and sit close to the pearl.

"That's better. Now, why have you come to see me?"

Nervously, I clear my throat before speaking.

"F-For months I've been miserable, but I don't know why. I have a good life, a good job, and a beautiful fiancée who loves me dearly. It started small but it grew to a point where I can't ignore it anymore. I'll lose everything if this hollowness persists. I was told to come here so that you could help me."

"I can see what you speak of. It is deeply entrenched in your soul and has been there much longer than you thought."

"Can you get rid of it?"

"I can but it will be a long and painful process. You will not leave this place the same as when you came. Are you prepared for this?"

"Yes. I'll do anything."

"Very good. Please take me into your hands and sit with me in your lap at the top of the stairs."

I throw off my backpack and do what I was told. Despite its size, the pearl is light as air. I gently carry it to the top of the stairs and sit down with my legs crossed. Along the edge of the lake, the fish begin to swim more violently while the sharks and whales turn towards the temple in anticipation. Before I can say anything, a pulse comes out from the pearl going through my body to the edge of the lake. In an instant, the sea creatures descend, flying above and below the water. The sky changes colors as cosmic clouds swirl around the stars. It's beautiful.

"Now we can begin," the pearl says, "Close your eyes and follow my voice."

I do so without hesitation. As soon as my eye lids close, the sounds of the splashing fish around me go mute. My muscles relax and my body feels weightless. From the darkness, a cloud forms in front of me. Vivid colors from the entire spectrum swirl around and dance in the otherwise black void. Some colors shone brightly while others drifted away, fading to grey.

"What is it?" I ask.

"This is everything that makes you," the pearl replies, "Your experiences, your emotions, your very soul. This exists in each person and there is never an identical match."

"It's incredible."

"Look up."

I do, zeroing in on a particular cloud. At first, all I can see is color, but when I look closer, I see movement. Familiar sounds gradually arose as I see my younger self being coached by my father as I rode my big boy bicycle for the first time in a bright yellow tint. In a shade of green, I see myself in my old trigonometry class, bored out of my mind, while in a different green I'm poking the web of a spider until it to falls on my head. In the far corner, there was a shade of dark blue where I stood with the rest of my family around my grandmother's bed, watching as she peacefully took her last breath. They interwove within each other seamlessly. A small smile stretched on my face while a tear formed in my eye.

"You remember these fondly?" The pearl asks.

"Some of them, except for my grandmother," I admit, "It's strange, but I hadn't thought about these moments for a long time. I wonder why."

"There's more. Look to your right."

Off to the side is a larger cloud of blues and violets. There's hardly a sound coming from this cluster, but my chest tightens with anxiety. Then came the sound of screeching tires and a scream. When I look, I see my younger self crying next to the flattened corpse of my old dog. Another scream, this time from my mother, in a different hue revealing the day we found out about my father staying at the office late at night with his younger coworker. More memories of sadness and despair unfold, each reveal weighs heavily on my heart as some tears fell.

"I... remember these," I say, "I don't want to look at these anymore. Let's go somewhere else."

"We will but do not dismiss these visions."

Together, we journey from one cloud to the next, traveling throughout the void, only stopping to reflect on the memories within each cluster. The deeper we travel, the more uncomfortable they become. Class presentations that turned my stomach, groundings that left me full of anger, the first time I got naked with someone I loved, the first time I was cheated on, the first time I had an affair. Every hideous betrayal I committed and every heartbreak I endured came back to me, reminding me of who I once was. In the middle of it all, I turn away in shame.

"Look up," the pearl commands.

"I can't," I murmur, "It's too much."

"All of this is who you are. You cannot escape it."

"That's not possible! There's no way that all of this is who I am. These are just memories."

"These unique experiences created the person you are today, for better or for worse. Rejecting them in favor of a lie to shield yourself from the truth will cause you pain."

"But I'm a different person now!"

"That may be true, but your refusal to acknowledge these memories out of shame has been tearing your soul apart. Look up. There is one more thing you must see."

I keep my head down; with everything that has been brought up, there was nothing that could counteract the slimy upset in my stomach.

"You mean it?"

That voice, I know it well. My head snaps up to see Maria in a golden, strawberry hue with half her face hidden in a pillow. Her bare shoulder peeked out from the clean white sheets I had at the time; her eyes sparkled in surprise and disbelief. All of the giddy, nervous sensations come back in full force. I can even feel my cheeks flush all over again.

".... Yeah."

"Say it again."

"Huh? Why?"

"I want to hear you say it again."

"....... I love you."

She continues to stare in amazement for a few moments. Then her beautiful lips stretched into a sweet smile, a smile I've worked so hard to see time and time again. She then buried her face into the pillows and I heard one final whisper.

"I'm so happy!"

A warm happiness fills my chest but is immediately tainted by a sickening dread. This woman, so beautiful and loving, gave herself to someone like me, a man riddled with flaws and regret. The more I stare into her adoring brown eyes, the more I understand. This was the moment where it all started. The moment I pushed all the ugliness into the pit of my subconscious for it to fester. All the hollowness and misery came from this moment, and I didn't even realize it. I remove a hand from the pearl to wipe away the tears.

"I did it for her," I whisper, "I just wanted to be a better man for her."

"You blocked out the worst parts of yourself to pretend to be who you wanted to be," the pearl hypothesizes, "But in your attempt to erase your past, those imperfect parts of yourself sat in the dark to rot and destroy."

Its words echo in my mind, etching themselves in my brain. All I can do is nod.

"Now what?" I ask.

"Now we must bring these memories together."

This was not what I expected to hear after everything I saw. The only thing I can mutter was a very confused "what?"

"We must bring these memories together."

"Do we have to?"

"We must if you really desire to cure yourself of the despair that has been plaguing you."

"It just- Do we have to unite all of them? Can't we destroy the worst ones? I don't know if I want to remember some of these things for the rest of my life."

"If I were to remove any one of these memories, it could leave a hole in your soul where the void can get in. You will slowly become a husk of a man who relies on temporary pleasures to endure life."

I listen carefully to these words. The conflict in my mind dies down as I understand.

"How do we do it?"

"You must accept all of these memories as they are and accept them all as a part of you," the pearl explains, "Be honest with yourself and this misery that has been bothering you will be subdued."

"Will this change who I am? Will it change what I want?"

"Perhaps. But it will bring you the peace that you desire."

This doesn't bring me any comfort, but I know I have to do it. For myself and Maria. My brow scrunches as I concentrate on the fragmented clouds around me. Every memory and emotion out there, I made my peace with, accepting them into my heart. As they come closer together, I become overwhelmed with everything. The clouds begin to melt into each other, turning into a technicolor kaleidoscope display. My face shifts between anger, sadness, delight, and embarrassment at such a rapid speed it's nauseating. Then, it all goes black. For some time, I sit in darkness contemplating everything that has happened. All is silent, all is calm. After a few seconds, a voice whispers in my ear.

"It is done."

I reopen my eyes and I'm back at the temple. The sky is still dark with the sea creatures floating around the island as if no time had passed. I blink once then twice to confirm where I am then look down at the pearl resting in my lap.

"What happened?" I ask.

"We are back in my realm," the pearl responds.

"But, what about what we just did?"

"What about it?"

"Where we were. It was- It was just so wonderful. How did we come back? What do I do now?"

"That I leave for you to decide."

"But the hollowness, the misery!"

"Do you feel it now?"

I pause to look up at the sky. I search my mind for a hint of what I felt before but there's nothing, not a trace of the misery or hollowness. I'm cured.

"I don't feel like myself. What does this mean? What am I supposed to do now? What about my life? What about Maria?"

"It would be best for you to determine that for yourself."

I look down at the pearl as it sits in my lap. My frustration and curiosity wants to squeeze it for answers, but contentment won me over. Without a word, I grasp the pearl in my hands and stand up. I walk back to the massive clam and place it back in the center.

"Life won't be the same now, will it?" I ask.

"It won't be," the pearl replies.

"It feels like I've been here for weeks."

"You have. Two weeks to be exact."

I'm shocked until my stomach grumbles. After a quick search, I find my backpack and tear it apart for food. The few protein bars I find in a side pocket are scarfed down in minutes. With my hunger satisfied, I sit in silence before looking back to the pearl in its perch.

"How will I explain this to everyone?" I ask.

"As I have said, I cannot advise you further. This is in your hands now."

For some reason, I'm fine with this answer. I pull my backpack onto my shoulders, give the pearl one last bow out of respect, then make my way back down to the lake; marching forward to a new future.

Bump in the Night

"Henry?"

A voice calling his name woke Henry Gibbons out of his slumber. Once he was somewhat conscious, he turned over to see his wife sitting up.

"Hm? What is it?" He grunted sleepily.

"I think I heard something downstairs," she whispered.

"You're just hearing things Maggie. Nothing and no one is downstairs," he said flatly before turning back over.

"Henry! There's someone downstairs. I know it!"

"You're letting your imagination get to you again. Go back to sleep."

"Henry Gibbons just listen!"

Henry groaned before sitting up. At first, he heard nothing but the usual creaking and moaning of their old house, sounds he had gotten comfortable with. One particular sputter reminded him to check the boiler in the morning. But just as he was about to lay back down, soft muttering came from down the hall. It started low and respectful but gradually harshened as the voices grew frustrated. Henry threw his head back and groaned.

"God dammit! I thought we finally got rid of them!" He whined.

"You mean there's a group down there? I thought they forgot about us," Maggie said.

"We haven't made an appearance in years! The rumors should have died down by now."

"Maybe some of the older children told them about us."

The voices downstairs continued to chatter, further grating on Henry's nerves.

"It's late. Maybe if we ignore them, they'll go home," Maggie suggested.

Henry grunted in agreement then shimmied back under the sheets. Trying desperately to return to dreamland, they lay completely still. Then a loud shout echoed, shattering their quiet night, with others joining in. Fed up, Henry threw off the covers.

"Damn sons of bitches!" He fumed as he pulled his bathrobe off the bedpost.

"Get back to bed Henry! If you go down there now, they'll tell all their friends and they'll keep coming back just like the last time," Maggie scolded.

"Someone needs to teach those little morons some manners!"

He shifted his body to sit on the side of his bed, nearly throwing off his back in the process. As he slid his feet into his slippers, he heard Maggie sit up and grab a book off her nightstand. A small twinge of shame got to him. She knew by now to let his stubbornness run its course; he knew this, and it depressed him. He stayed on the bedside, contemplating going back to sleep and forgetting his mission. Maggie opened her paperback mystery novel then spoke.

"Go ahead if it will make you feel better."

The complacency in her voice added to the anger already brewing inside him. Henry stood up and stormed out of the room, leaving Maggie to her reading. As he made his way down the hall, stomping on every creaky floorboard to the top of the stairs. The shouting quieted down to murmurs. The brief thought of retreat entered his mind while the normal sounds of the house took over. Perhaps his ruckus was enough, and he could go back to a peaceful rest.

"Come on out you motherfucker!"

One glide down the stairs and Henry was standing in front of a group of four teenagers, two boys and two girls. The boy who was standing with his arms open fell down at his sudden arrival. All eyes were locked on him. A cardboard Ouija board was laid out on the dusty ground in the center of their circle. He made a mental note to sweep later. Henry waiting for someone to speak up but when all he got were blank stares, he stepped forward.

"Well, what do you want?" He demanded.

No one on the ground was brave enough to speak.

"Do you have any idea how late it is? We're trying to sleep here!"

One girl scooted closer to the other girl wearing a soccer jersey while the boy who was shouting crawled backwards. Henry tapped his foot out of irritation.

"Well? Do you have anything to say for yourselves? Huh? Come on, speak up!"

Finally, the lanky boy off to the side coughed.

"Who are you?" He asked, still quivering.

"I'm the homeowner!" Henry snapped back, "And you kids are trespassing on my property!"

The lanky boy blinked in confusion then turned to the others in the group. They stared at each other before Lanky looked back at him.

"Um, sir? No one has lived in this house for decades," he explained.

"That's because I'm still here, smartass! And I don't like late night company!"

While the children continued to gawk at him, Henry squinted to get a better idea of what he was dealing with. None of them looked older than sixteen. The girl who was hiding wore heavy makeup and shivered while the sporty girl tried to look stoic. The troublemaking idiot crawling away wore an obnoxious, flamboyantly colored t-shirt with random cartoon characters on it and sweatpants. Then he returned to Lanky with a stern look that he hadn't used in a long time.

"Is anyone going to tell me why you kids are on my property?" He demanded.

Lanky was about speak but shrunk back under his stern gaze. Then Pretty popped her head from behind Sporty's broad shoulders.

"W-we were trying to communicate with g-ghosts sir," she squeaked, "We heard this place was haunted so we came t-t-to try and talk to the spirits."

All Henry could do was sigh, this was just the answer he was expecting. He crossed his arms and loomed over them.

"Well, you met one. Now piss off!" He barked.

All the teenagers' expressions went from fear to bewilderment. Pretty and Lanky exchanged looks while Sporty and Idiot refused to take their eyes off of him.

"Y-you're the ghost?" Sporty finally asked.

"Yeah, one of them," Henry replied.

"So, the séance worked?"

She pointed to the Ouija board with a shaky hand. Henry raised an eyebrow.

"What? That stupid thing? That didn't wake me up. Your shouting and screaming was what woke me and my wife up. What time is it anyway?"

Out of habit, he looked over to the grandfather clock that stood in the corner but the frozen hands and rusted face told him nothing.

"I-it's 2:38 a.m. sir," Pretty said.

He looked back at her to see a small rectangle thing in her hand that glowed.

"What's that?" He asked.

"What?"

"That thing in your hand."

"This?"

Pretty held out the glowing rectangle that showed the time in front of a picture of her and Idiot's faces.

"Yes, that. What is it?" Henry asked again.

"It's an Iphone," she replied.

"A phone?"

"Yeah but you can use it for other things."

"Like what?"

Her posture relaxed as she scooted away from Sporty.

"Um, well, you can take pictures with it and watch videos," Pretty explained as best she could.

"So, you just put a camera, a television, and a phone all in one thing?"

"Kinda."

"They replaced televisions with this?"

"Well, no, not really."

"Then why do you need that thing for? It's too small to watch anything."

"Um, it's nice to have that stuff everywhere-"

"Why?"

"Uh...."

She turned to her friends for help but they were equally at a loss for words. For a few minutes she pondered before replying.

"You can search for all kinds of information on here!"

"We old folks call that a library," Henry shot back, "Don't you kids read books anymore?"

"Yeah, but sometimes we don't want to read..."

It took a few seconds for her to realize what she just said. She gave a pathetic half-smile and scooted behind Sporty again. Henry shook his head.

"You all are like Jeremy, always wanting the hot new gadget for no good reason," he bemoaned.

"Jeremy?" Lanky asked.

"He lives in the upstairs bathroom. Died back it '75. Nice kid but a bit of an airhead."

"Wait. How many ghosts are in this place?" Sporty piped up.

Henry paused and looked off into the distance while counting on his fingers. After starting over three or four times, he looked back at her.

"About twelve or sixteen," he replied.

The group gasped.

"Wait a minute, hold on. There are sixteen ghosts in here? Why?" Sporty asked, trying to comprehend what she heard.

"They lose their homes and come here to stay until they find another place," Henry explained, "I'm their landlord."

"Landlord?" Lanky piped up.

"Yeah, Maggie and I don't mind having them stay. Times are hard these days."

The teens looked between the specter in front of them to each other. This was clearly not the haunting they were expecting. Henry sighed, relinquishing his hardened façade, then looked over to Pretty.

"What time is it again?" He asked.

She looked down at her glowing phone.

"It's 2:48," she replied.

"Alright. Pack up your spirit board crap and go home. Your parents won't be happy if they find out you've been out this late."

Sporty and Lanky gave him a quick nod then started to fold up the Ouija board while Pretty sat still trying to decide if she was satisfied or underwhelmed. Henry over saw their packing until they were almost done then turned back to the stairs. Just as he was about to take the first step up, he heard someone scramble to their feet.

"Hold on! I have a question!"

The cockiness in the tone made him grimace. He turned to see Idiot standing in the middle of the room. The others stopped what they were doing to watch, with Pretty looking particularly concerned.

"What do you want?" Henry grumbled.

"Are you old man Gibbons?" Idiot inquired.

"Oh Jesus Christ! I thought everyone forgot about me already!"

Despite his annoyance, the response made Idiot's face light up.

"I told you guys!" He shouted back to his friends, "My uncle told me all about this dude!"

Henry groaned then turned to face him.

"Okay, so is it true that-"

Idiot's line of questioning was cut off by Henry's raised hand.

"No, I did not murder my wife in her sleep. No, I did not chop her up then hang myself. No, I did not murder any school children and bury them in my backyard. Yes, I did frighten someone to death but that was an accident and she had a weak heart to begin with. No, I do not go looking to scare people. I just want to be left alone."

With his monologue done, he leaned on the stair railing, looking at Idiot right in the eye. The young boy's eyes bulged out so much he thought they would pop.

"I've heard it all before," Henry explained, "Now, if you don't mind, I'd like to go back to sleep. So please leave."

He was about to go but was stopped yet again by the solitary shuffling of Idiot.

"Well, I have one more question," he said, snickering.

Both Sporty and Lanky's eyes widened while Pretty shook her head slowly.

"Well, I was just wondering if you have, like, powers, you know?" Idiot asked.

"I do. What's your point?"

"Drew, don't do it man," Lanky warned.

"So, could you, like, sneak into a chick's room and fuck her without her even knowing?"

Everyone in the room went silent. The usual house noises filled the dead air while Henry processed what was just asked. The other teens looked away in embarrassment and disgust while Idiot continued to smile confidently. Once the question finally hit, Henry's face twisted into a hideous scowl and his hands clenched into fists.

"What did you say?" He hissed through his teeth.

Instantly, the smug grin on Idiot's face fell. Pretty ducked back behind Sporty again. Henry left his spot on the stairs to walk up to the dumb boy. Once he was toe to toe with him, he gritted his teeth into snarl. Idiot leaned back in response.

"What did you just ask me?" Henry repeated, his voice becoming more inhuman.

Idiot opened his mouth, but nothing came out; all he could do was blubber. Henry's form grew to tower over the trembling kid, his teeth becoming long and pointed while his eyes darkened into black voids. A growing wet spot appeared in the crotch of Idiot's sweatpants.

"Get. Out. Now!" Henry ordered.

A certain foul smell filled up the room, causing Pretty to cover her nose. Idiot remained glued to his spot before giving him a single nod before backing up. Sporty and Lanky picked everything up and the group to rush towards the door. Before they could exit, a skeletal hand reached up from the floor boards to grab Pretty by the ankle. She shrieked while Sporty tried to kick it but another pair of boney hands came out from the wall to grab her.

Two glowing green skeletons appeared from their hiding places to leer at the group with chattering teeth. The Ouija board was dropped as the group ran out of the house screaming, zooming down the abandoned driveway to the nearby suburb. The skeletons cackled as they morphed back into their true forms: Tom Higgs and Barry Dome, former football stars of '87. Henry fumed for another minute before shifting back to normal.

"That was amazing! Did you see their faces?" Barry wheezed.

"We had the one kid pissing his pants!" Tom added, "I can't remember the last time we did that!"

"Actually, that one was my doing," Henry corrected.

The two ghosts looked back at him.

"Really? Geez Mr. Gibbs, I didn't know you still had it in you. I thought you retired from all this," Barry said.

"I did! Then those brats showed up," Henry replied.

"Ah, I was wondering what you were doing up so late."

"You okay Mr. Gibbs?" Tom asked, looking down at the older ghost's clenched fists.

Henry took in a deep breath and forced his hands to relax.

"I'm fine," he said, "Just angered by what the last one asked me."

"What'd he say?" Barry asked.

"Never mind. Just go back to sleep."

"We can go after them if you'd like. It's been a while since we've haunted someone," Tom offered.

"No, no. They're just young idiots who've had enough spooks for the night. Just forget about them."

"Alright Mr. Gibbs."

With that the boys vanished within the walls. Henry leaned backwards to crack his back before shuffling up the stairs. When he reached the top, the bathroom door opened, and a naked man poked his head out while clutching a toaster.

"What's all the commotion?" He asked.

"It's nothing Jeremy. Just some late-night visitors," Henry explained tiredly.

"Really? It's been a long time since we've had ghost hunters here," Jeremy remarked, "You think they'll be back?"

"I hope not! I'm too old for this crap!"

"Ha-ha, yeah! I don't think I'm ready for another wave of visitors either. It gets more awkward by the year having someone burst in while I'm in the tub."

"You should have thought about that before ending it in the buff."

"I wasn't expecting the afterlife to be like this!"

A high-pitched barking silenced them as an old Yorkie ran cheerfully towards them.

"There you are Peaches," Henry cooed, stooping down to pick the dog up, "Where have you been all day?"

Peaches panted happily then licked his nose.

"Wherever she was, it looks like she had fun," Jeremy chuckled, "Hey, are we still doing poker night tomorrow?"

"From what I understand, yes. I think Caroline wanted to do a poetry reading too."

Jeremy groaned.

"Are we really going to humor her? She's shit."

"I heard that!" A voice screamed from the door across the way.

"Whatever," Jeremy sighed, "G' night Mr. Gibbons."

"Goodnight."

The bathroom door closed, and Henry continued down the hall with the happy Yorkie in his arms. When he approached his bedroom, he peered through the door crack to gage the mood inside. Maggie sat quietly in bed with her paperback, the irritation from before had evaporated as she immersed herself in the crisp yellow pages. Henry pushed the door open to enter. She glanced up from her book then looked at the dog in his arms.

"You found Peaches!" She exclaimed, "Where was she?"

"Running around, as usual," Henry replied.

He sat on the bedside and allowed Peaches to hop out of his embrace. The Yorkie went right over to Maggie's side and snuggled into her arm. She marked her page then put the book back on the side table while Henry hung his robe on the bedpost before getting under the covers.

"How did everything go?" She asked as she scratches Peaches' chin.

"Fine up until the last question," Henry replied as he rested his head on the pillow, "In all my years on this Earth, I will never understand why the living feel the need to ask about my sexual prowess as a ghost."

"Oh dear. You didn't hurt them, did you?"

"No. Just scared them. I know you don't like it when I get physical."

As much as he wanted to get comfortable in his own bed, his restless mind kept him staring at the ceiling. Maggie continued to sit, knowing there was more to be said. She didn't have to wait long.

"Why me? Why did I have to stay behind? Why couldn't they get someone younger to do this? I've got no reason to stay on this crummy planet and I'm getting tired of this ghost business. I want to move on too! Why the hell should either of us still be here?"

With his outburst over, he let his head sink into his pillow. Maggie waited for an addendum, but when none came, she placed a hand onto his shoulder.

"Whatever the reason, we're in this together," she whispered.

A warm smile spread in Henry's face.

"What did I ever do to deserve you?" He muttered.

She smiled back then leaned over to kiss his cheek before shimmying under the covers herself. Peaches made her way to the foot of the bed in between them before curling up into a ball to rest for the night.

Thank you for reading.

I'll see you in the next one!

Made in the USA
Middletown, DE
04 June 2023